HUNTER

BEHOLDEN TO BALANCE, BOOK 3

CILLA RAVEN

Cover art and design by
Nichole W. - Rainy Day Artwork

Get new release updates and exclusive content when you sign up for my mailing list!

I dedicate this book...

To anyone who has ever felt like their back was up against the wall and life just never had your back.
To every person who had to pull themselves out of their own 'dark place' and work like hell to stay out.
To all the ones who think they're broken, even when it's that brokenness that makes you who you are.
This book is for you.

To everyone who read Initiate and Reign and decided to read this one too, this book is for you.

To my great, amazing, fantastic, wonderful, awesome husband who inspires me each and every day.

You can skip the bad words and dirty parts in this one too, Mawmaw. I love you!

CONTENTS

PART I
HELL'S TRIALS

CHAPTER 1

BECKS

*P*anic and insurmountable fear, sharp and potent in their intensity, spread through my senses as Hell consumed me. It swallowed me whole after Absinthe waved his hand in front of my face, sending me straight to the gauntlet with zero hesitation and even less warning.

I felt like I was falling, like all my nerve endings were alight with jitters of terror, as the tethers I'd had to Earth and my previous life snapped. My connections with Brax and the rest of my teammates shattered one by one like they were made of glass, obliterated as if they never existed in the first place.

Then there was the heat.

It licked against every inch of my skin, so hot it was nearly unbearable, but somehow, the air around me just kept getting hotter. I could feel sweat forming and then evaporating, not only on my brow, but everywhere. As if, wherever I was, the atmosphere was squeezing me dry like a too wet sponge left out in the sun of a desert.

I couldn't move my arms.

They were held tightly by something, but I couldn't tell what it was since all I could see was impenetrable and endless blackness everywhere. My body was shaking about sporadically, and with each spasm, my back, head, and legs pounded against something hard and cold, the contrast in the heat and the cold shocking me even further.

Twisting and turning, trying to get the heat to cool, the cold to warm, the shaking to stop, and the fear to settle, a cry of pain and anguish ripped through my throat. The sound landed in my ears with no echo to speak of bouncing back at me, my surroundings swallowing even sound itself.

I was able to roll to my side despite whatever was going on. Still, the motion only made things worse, a prospect I hadn't thought was possible until it was too late, and another scream escaped me.

Bright white fluorescent light overwhelmed all my senses for a second, and as I tried to blink through it, a man's voice said, "Ms. Mason, we've talked about this."

Strong hands grabbed me by each of my biceps and pulled me to my feet. "This kind of behavior will not be tolerated. Do you want us to sedate you again?"

I was in a padded room...

The padded room I had tried to avoid at all costs while growing up in Quarry Hill Children's Behavioral Health Center, and standing there before me, was Dr. Hapson...

The Dr. Hapson, whose signature solution to nonconforming, out of control psychos, had always involved the sharp end of a needle and a hefty high.

A straight jacket, locked firmly in place by well-practiced hands, confined my arms to my sides tightly. When I looked down and saw the offensive garment, realization started to take hold of me.

I hadn't been falling.

I wasn't feeling pain or heat or cold.

All of that had to have just been the effects of coming out of a really intense high.

'*But that would mean.....*,' I thought as I glanced back up at Dr. Hapson with dazed and confused eyes, an entirely new fear gripping me.

'*None of it was real?*'

Immediately, Brax's scary, beautiful face bounded to the forefront of my mind, right along with everyone else's I'd met over the past few weeks.

Derrick.

Tyler.

Adam.

Absinthe.

Philippa.

With each flash of a face, a new and agonizing pain seared through my chest.

Ava, Otto, Fergus, Tina, Brandt, Logan, Benjamin, the Mer queen, Queen Agatha of the fairies, and one of her daughters, Saleem, King Preston of the pixies.

What about all the time before Brax showed up? Was my time in the halfway house just a hallucination too? Was Ava just a figment of my imagination? For that matter, what about Rick and everything he did to me? Or what I did to him because of it? I couldn't have imagined the pain and suffering that followed that night without actually having lived it! Even my imagination, stoked with hallucinogens, isn't that dark, creative, or accurate.

'*It couldn't have all been fake! There's no way! No fucking way!*' I thought as my breath started heaving like I couldn't take in enough air to satisfy my panicked body.

"Ms. Mason," Dr. Hapson said warningly as he moved his hands to rest on his hips. "You need to calm down. I'm here to let you out, so the worst parts are already over."

But I just couldn't believe what was happening. I couldn't, even for a second, entertain the idea that everything I'd been through wasn't real.

I wouldn't.

"There's been a mistake," I said as I tried to get my breathing back under control.

'Something has gone terribly wrong,' I tried to rationalize with myself. *'Maybe Absinthe messed up. I mean, I know my powers don't exactly listen to me. Maybe his powers give him just as much of a headache as mine do sometimes.'*

Dr. Hapson shook his head at me with a disappointed look before he nodded to the orderlies that were still holding me by my biceps. Each of them stepped toward me and started unbuckling the clasps on the straight jacket, and the relief I felt when it was finally off pushed a sigh between my lips.

"No more attacking the orderlies, Ms. Mason, or you will be put right back in here. Do you understand me?" Dr. Hapson asked as if I had any idea about what he was referring to.

I had never, not even when I was *supposed* to be in this God-forsaken place, attacked an orderly.

I knew better than that.

'Just play it cool, Becks,' I told myself. *'Go along with whatever's happening right now, and when you get an opportunity, make a break for it and try to find Brax and the guys. They'll be able to help.'*

"Yes, sir," I said in my best placating tone, which had the desired effect of making Dr. Hapson breathe forcefully through his nose as his lips pursed, and he turned his back on me.

He led me through the all too familiar hallways where I spent most of my childhood, his keys clanking against his leg in the pocket of his white lab coat with every step he took. The orderlies were following silently behind me, caging me between them and Dr. Hapson.

Everything was the same as the last time I was here, but there was no doubt in my mind that I was irrevocably different.

There were still the ever-present, lingering aromas of sanitizer and surgical-grade alcohol, mixed with the same familiar notes of sadness, anxiety, and fear in the air. Children could still be eyed through the small square windows on each of the rooms we passed. Even though they were probably all different children than those that were here while I was, they looked exactly the same as those I had known before.

This place affected a child's demeanor and psyche like that, making them sorry excuses for the children they once were before they came to this place.

It broke them.

However, I wasn't broken.

Not anymore.

As I looked inside myself, reaching to where I knew my power lived, I felt it there, my purplish-blue power, wrapping around and protecting my soul just as it had in my memories. In fact, it felt stronger and more potent than it ever had before, so I couldn't for the life of me understand how I was back in the asylum instead of Hell.

'What a crazy thought to have, worrying about why I'm not in Hell,' I nearly chuckled at myself. Luckily, I stopped the laughter before it could leave me because if it had, Dr. Hapson would've had another reason to think I'm insane and in need of his special attention.

I couldn't see outside since we were on the third floor, which didn't sport any windows, so there was no telling what time it was. If I knew that critical piece of information, I would've had a better chance of figuring out how to break out of here, given the fact that I knew this place ran like a well-oiled machine, never missing a deadline.

"What time is it, Doctor?" I asked as we turned a corner while Dr. Hapson held the door to the staircase open for me.

"It's six p.m. I took you out just in time for dinner."

The way he said that made it sound like he was my knight in shining armor, thinking so much of me and my welfare that he deigned to let me out so I could make it to dinner on time.

'Well, how fucking thoughtful of you.' I rolled my eyes with disgust at the back of his head as he descended the stairs before me.

We were soon walking off the staircase and onto the first floor, where I knew we would pass through the brightly lit and open reception area to get to the cafeteria. I'd never tried to escape through the doors there before. Still, I'd always thought that particular location was a weakness for the asylum because it was monitored loosely.

The doors open automatically as patients are led to the cafeteria on the other side of the large building for every meal. It was cruel, really, those doors opening and closing as we were passed by them like cattle being herded to another pasture, six times a day. Six times a day for ten years, I'd been directed to ignore those doors and the freedom they could offer and solely focus on 'getting better.'

Well, that wasn't going to happen again. Not today.

As we got closer to the doors, a plan quickly began to develop in my mind.

If I could just go along without alerting anyone to what I was thinking or give them a reason to worry, I could literally run right out the front door.

The only security guard in the whole place was sitting behind the reception desk. If I could tap into my power while I ran, there would be no way he'd be able to catch me.

I remembered the bus trip from the asylum to the halfway house well, seeing as how it had been my first time off of the asylum's grounds in ten years; things like that always seemed to have a way of sticking around.

The outside of the asylum beyond the parking lot was nothing but well-manicured grass and neatly trimmed hedges lining the road that led to it for a pretty good distance. However, after a short time, the bus I'd taken had sped through a forest that butted up against the street thickly.

If I could make it to the forest without getting caught, I'd be free again.

I could start my search for Brax and my teammates, and we could start trying to figure out what went wrong. I could rip Absinthe a new one for attempting to send me to the gauntlet so unprepared in the first place. For that matter, I could also tear him apart for messing the task up as well.

These thoughts raced through my mind as I got closer to the front door, anxiety and excitement building within me with every step that brought me closer to freedom. My power seemed to be excited too, almost as if it knew it was about to be tapped into, and it just couldn't wait to be used to help me escape.

I grabbed it in my mind in preparation, and it shivered at the connection I'd made with it, causing a smile to spread across my face.

My power had my back, and I knew it wouldn't let me down, so as the perfect moment of opportunity came within sight, I tapped into my power and threw my feet into the floor.

I propelled myself toward the sliding glass door with everything I had in me, only realizing a moment too late that since I'd moved so fast, the automatic sensor that was supposed to open the door for me hadn't even registered that I'd moved toward it.

Stepping back at a normal human speed, I finally got the sensor to see me. However, those were a few seconds I couldn't afford to lose since, within the next beat of my heart, the orderlies were grabbing me and trying to pull me back away from the doors.

My thoughts raced as I felt an unprecedented amount of panic shoot through me for the second time within the last half hour. Images of the years I'd spent in the asylum bombarded my psyche, an overwhelming sense of sadness attached to each and every memory that was made here.

My time at this asylum was supposed to be done. Though I knew I'd be living with the effects this place had on me for the rest of my life, there was no doubt in my mind that if I let the orderlies take me, I'd never get back out again.

Something was trying to tell me what to do, trying to guide me with unspoken but thorough knowledge of the future, and I knew instantly that I'd be a fool not to listen to the instinctive voice. It was telling me to get out as quickly as possible, no matter what it took to do so.

"No!" I screamed as the orderlies made contact with my skin, and suddenly, without my consent, my power burst out of me because I was still holding onto it.

The orderlies were flung away from me, the glass in the windows and doors shattered, and alarms started to blare their protest as the lights flashed red throughout the building. I chanced a glance back behind me, and what I saw sent an insane amount of fear through me.

The orderlies', Dr. Hapson's, and even the unsuspecting security guard's bodies were all in pieces, scattered about the bright white reception area. It made the whole room look like a well-written, blood-spattered gorefest had taken place, rather than just a simple escape attempt.

For a moment, I couldn't hear any sounds, all my coherent thoughts ceasing their constant flow through my mind, as even my heart felt like it'd stopped beating altogether.

Red and white made up my new landscape, the drops and smears and splatters and chunks of flesh painting the canvas before me like Death himself had come a-calling.

No part of the people that had just been living, breathing, healthy organisms only moments before were recognizable anymore, and my body shuddered as I took it all in.

As my chest began to heave, and my heart started back up again, a single thought broke forth through my consciousness:

'What have I done?'

'THEY WERE INNOCENT!' My internal monologue started up full force, a self-hatred starting to form solidly in the pit of my stomach. *'They were just doing their jobs, and now look at them! There's hardly even a 'them' left now!'*

Heat scorched my cheeks as a tingling sensation spread across my skin, and my throat got so thick it was hard to breathe normally.

I couldn't rationalize what I'd done... no... what my power had done.

That wasn't me.

I didn't kill like that.

I mean, the way I killed Rick had been pretty brutal, but it was nothing compared to what I was facing now, and let's be honest... Rick deserved so much more than what I'd done to him. These people, though? The worst they'd done was to be in the wrong place at the wrong time.

'I can't stay here,' the thought tore through my mind like a spike of dread-filled ice piercing my soul, cold and foreboding. I couldn't ignore it, even if I'd wanted to.

I turned around, surprised my body was actually listening to me for once. With a heavy weight of guilt spreading through my chest, I grabbed hold of my power again. I started running for the door frame, glass crunching under my standard, asylum issued, white sneakers as I made my way out into the sunshine.

However, when I was outside the building, squinting as the sun streamed into my eyes, my surroundings changed, the world morphing and falling into itself.

Again, I found myself in blackness, that eerily familiar feeling I'd had when I woke up in the asylum, assaulting me all over again.

'What the actual fuck?' My hands involuntarily reached for my head in desperation because the tremendous pounding I felt beating against my brain was so intense.

Then I felt the sharp sting of the belt across my back and around my arm, my heart seizing inside my chest as a voice I thought I'd never have to hear again screamed down at me.

"Why can't you just be normal?" my adoptive mother yelled as my adoptive father reared back to send another swipe of the belt my way.

His hand was wrapped tightly around the brown leather strap that had horses running down its center, leaving the belt buckle to act as the worst kind of punctuation mark as it whipped through the air to land wherever it ended up.

I was curled up on my toddler bed, huddled in the fetal position with my hands trying their best to protect my face and head from the blows I knew wouldn't stop coming.

The beatings had never stopped when *I'd* had enough.

Only when *they* grew too exasperated to continue their torment would I find any relief. Honestly, sometimes the healing bruises hurt more than they did while receiving the blows that made them.

'Something's not right,' I thought as I tried to make myself into a smaller target. 'I shouldn't be here.'

"You only say those things because you want to get a rise out of us," my adoptive mother wailed as I fought to hold onto what was real and what wasn't. "Well, the world doesn't revolve around you, Rebecca! When are you ever going to get that through your head?"

"I'm sorry," I heard my voice plead as tears started falling unchecked from my eyes. "I'm sorry! I won't visit the fairies anymore, I promise, Mommy!"

Another blow landed then, the buckle smashing right into the front of my shin, where my legs were curled up against my chest.

"Fairies aren't real, Rebecca," my adoptive father's calm, low voice said in stark contrast to the angry lashing he was giving me.

'Why am I the only one that can see them?' my thoughts wandered as the beating and screaming continued. 'They wouldn't do this to me if they could see them! I just wanted to play with them. They're my friends. I talked to them, so they have to be real!'

'Hold on...,' reason finally started to break through the childhood fears that were holding me captive. 'I don't live here anymore. This isn't my life now. These people are dead.'

I took my hands from my head and stood up to my full adult height, noting quickly that I was indeed, not a child at the mercy to the whims of my adoptive parents anymore. The looks on their faces when I leveled them with what was probably the most hate-filled glare I'd ever produced in my life were absolutely priceless.

'You'll never have a chance so sweet as this again, Becksy baby,' a voice I didn't wholly recognize said sweetly in my mind, as fantasized images of me taking that horse belt from my adoptive father's hands danced through my train of thought.

'They're so weak compared to us,' the voice continued as I found my feet moving of their own accord, stalking toward my adoptive parents. With every step I took, they tried to back away, fear growing in their eyes as a satisfaction I'd never felt in my life, seeped through my senses, a low, slow laugh that was both my own and not, sounding from my throat.

'That's right, Becksy baby,' she said, urging me ever forward. 'Hand over the reins and let your power handle this.'

A small sliver of warning tingled through my mind, but it was short-lived and fleeting. As I saw my hand whip out and grab the belt from my adoptive father's hand, my laugh got louder, entirely my own this time.

'I've waited so long for this,' I heard a voice say in my head, but I couldn't tell whether it was my voice or my power's, and right then, I didn't care either way.

CHAPTER 2

BRAX

"What the ever titty-loving fuck, Absinthe?" I screamed at the jinn while I stared at the spot Becks just disappeared from.

"What?" that fucking psycho said, looking up at me as if he had no idea what he'd done to piss me off, his purple eyes big and round at my outburst.

At that, Tyler exploded into his wolf form, right there in the middle of the living room of the beach safe house, pulling everyone's attention to him. His gigantic frame toppled an end table with his tail, the glass from the lamp that'd been sitting there, shattering and scattering everywhere across the floor.

A feral growl tore from his throat as he lunged toward Absinthe. Even though he knocked them both to the floor and looked to be fully intent on ripping Absinthe's jugular from his neck, it was like he just couldn't get his teeth to bite down as Becks' alpha order stopped Tyler's beast in his tracks.

"Woah, boy," Absinthe said around a chuckle, his hands raised in surrender. "You don't have to be upset. None of you do." His eyes drifted over each of us, a smile still curving his lips. "Sending Becks to the gauntlet was the best thing for everyone."

I hardly got a chance to process his words before a familiar and dreaded heat started searing through my chest. As I watched, knowing what was happening, I saw that the guys around me were feeling it too.

A groan from Adam and Derrick, a surprised huff from Absinthe, and a whimper from Tyler's wolf reached my ears as my hands went to my chest, all of our connections with Becks incinerating as she fully descended into Hell.

I'd felt that feeling before when my last familiar, Roland, had entered the gauntlet. The pain of losing my connection with Becks was just as powerful and soul-shattering as I remembered from the last time I'd felt it.

However, I didn't know Becks already shared some sort of connection with Absinthe, so his reaction surprised the hell out of me. But it was apparent there was something between them because he seemed to be experiencing the same break from her as the rest of Dragon team was.

That whole concept pissed me off even more as the heat inside my chest started to dissipate, leaving a lonely and gaping hole in its place.

He'd tied himself to her so thoroughly that he and Becks were now just as inexplicably linked as I was to her.

A protective/jealous/fearful/hatred combo, so maddeningly thick it might as well have been lava, spread through me at the thought, consuming me whole. If it hadn't been for Becks' alpha order, I would've done everything in my power to tear Absinthe's entire existence from this world.

"What was that?" Derrick asked, only barely pulling my attention from all the different ways I wanted to end Absinthe.

The looks on all of their faces had my anger dying off and my empathy skyrocketing instantly.

Derrick looked like he couldn't understand what was going on at all. Adam seemed close to tears as his hands gripped the shirt he was wearing at chest level, his eyes glazing over as if he'd just been thrust into another vision. Absinthe was looking down at his own chest with his head tilted to the side as if he couldn't comprehend pain in the first place.

But it was Tyler's beast that really got me in the feels.

He'd backed up off of Absinthe, all of his legs bent and tail tucked as the saddest whimper I'd ever heard in my life continued to escape him. He rolled over onto his side as his eyes searched the space around him, presumably looking for an explanation for what he was feeling.

A few seconds later, he shifted back into his human form. It was apparent that his beast could not handle the loss of his connection with Becks, so he'd handed his control back over to Tyler.

Tyler looked just as pained as his beast had, but upon realizing he was back and everyone was looking at him, he tried his best to play it off as he stood up, showing an impassive front meant to hide how he felt from us. However, I still knew how he really felt because our connection was still intact.

"Brax, what was that?" Derrick asked again.

Turning my eyes to him from Tyler, I said, "It was our connection with Becks breaking when she got to Hell. She can't be tied to anyone, not even her familiar, while she's in the gauntlet. The powers that be think those connections will influence her too much, so they strip her of them when she gets there. You guys weren't attached to someone when you went through the gauntlet. You didn't have familiars either, so you didn't feel it when you went, but you can bet your ass Becks just felt it; probably worse than any of us because she didn't lose just one connection. She lost five."

Derrick and Tyler looked at each other like they were confused for a second before they each turned their attention to Absinthe, having come to the same realization as I had. It seemed like they weren't any happier about Absinthe's connection with Becks than I was.

16

Absinthe stood up from the floor, still looking dazed from what'd happened. Soon enough, he glanced up to see all of us staring him down, except for Adam, who was still lost in whatever vision he was having.

"What's your plan, huh?" Derrick said, walking over and getting right in Absinthe's face again. "What are you playing at, sending Becks to the gauntlet when there's no way in all the realms she's ready for it?"

Absinthe bent his knees a little and sent his hands out to the sides as he said, "But she *is* ready for it."

Tyler stepped up right beside Derrick then and asked, "How do you figure that, huh?"

Absinthe stood up straight and clasped his hands together in front of him as a small smile spread across his face that didn't reach his eyes. Sighing a deep breath, he turned around and walked to the kitchen island, ignoring the chairs at the bar entirely as he hopped up onto the counter, leveling each of us with a sympathetic look on his face.

"I'll answer that in about a minute when Adam comes back to us," Absinthe finally responded, and I just couldn't dwell on how he knew precisely when Adam's vision would be over.

Derrick, Tyler, and I stood there, fuming the entire minute, not very patiently. When Adam finally came out of his vision looking like he'd just seen something that threw him off, I tried to penetrate his mind and see what he'd seen, but it was of no use. He'd learned how to block his thoughts from me, and until he wanted them known, there was no hope of me finding out what he saw.

"Fuck!" Adam yelled as his anger made him ball his fists in front of him and tighten every muscle on his body. Really, he looked like he was going to explode from the pressure buildup as he yelled, "Aaaaaaaa! Does it ever fucking end?"

I'd never seen him so angry or heard him yell like that, even in everyone's memories, and I know my eyebrows nearly reached my hairline as I regarded him.

It seemed like Tyler and Derrick were just as surprised at his outburst as I was, but Absinthe was just sitting there on the counter as if he expected it all along.

"Hey, bud," Absinthe said to Adam in a calming tone I scoffed at. "I know that's not how it's going to go down. Okay? Just forget about that vision."

Adam's eyes were bugging out of his head as he glared at Absinthe. "And I should just trust you on that?"

Absinthe didn't seem fazed by the question, but he also didn't answer, almost as if he knew Adam wasn't done. Adam threw his hands out to the side and continued, "Why should we do that, huh? You're a jinn! Immortal! Why would you ever care about Becks or us when you're going to outlive all of us? We're nothing but specks on the eternal timeline for you, and that's it!"

Absinthe sighed deeply before he answered, all of us hanging on every word he said.

"I know you guys think I'm the bad guy, that simply because I'm immortal, I have nothing to lose and no reason to care, but you're wrong. I do care about you guys and Becks despite how short our time together may be. Whether all of our lives end in the apocalypse or if we all live to ripe old ages, that fact won't change.

I've seen the future, just as you have, but I've seen more versions of it than you, so when I tell you that you need to forget that vision, please believe me. I wouldn't steer you wrong on purpose."

I don't think any of us were convinced by his words, but even I couldn't deny how genuine he sounded.

"As for how I knew Becks was ready for the gauntlet, that's a bit of a longer story," he said as his gaze drifted over all of us. "Look at it this way..." He shifted how he was sitting on the counter and moved his hands while he talked.

"The world is in absolute chaos right now, right?"

I don't know if anyone nodded to him in response, but he continued on as if we all had. "Right. Even the human world is going crazy. Toilet paper, masks... I mean, I don't know how often you guys look at the humans while you're policing the creatures in their world, but they're feeling it too, let me tell ya."

Absinthe sighed dejectedly but kept going. "Anyway, well... Every species, in every realm, no matter how large, small, powerful, or weak they are, they're all feeling the looming apocalypse because it's closer to happening now than it ever has been before. It's why none of you hunters can rest easy, why everything feels so chaotic right now. Because as 'doomsday' as it sounds, that's really what we're facing here."

Crossing my arms over my chest with a huff, I said, "All of us already knew that, dipshit. What does any of that have to do with Becks being ready for the gauntlet or not?" I was surprised I could actually articulate a straight question given how angry I was, but somehow, I made it happen.

"What I'm getting at is this: the world can't sustain its existence by running the same way as it has since the last king and his queens died off. Or, should I say, were killed before their time had come."

"What are you talking about now? Get to the fucking point soon or so help me..." Tyler said as his body started shaking again.

Absinthe jumped down from the counter, his clothes jingling as he moved while he sent a pleading look at all of us. "Look, kings and queens were always supposed to rule over the hunters. It was the only way to maintain the balance: by ensuring that the most powerful and balanced among you ran things, that each of them were able to keep the others grounded so they could sustain their power and rule justly.

However, some hunters weren't happy with their lot, those that wanted all the power for themselves. So, they took it.

These hunters, they basically gathered a group of like-minded individuals together and formed a secret society. They called themselves 'The Order of Division,' and their mission was simple: to kill the future kings and queens before the rest of the hunters ever even knew they existed, so they could separate out and manipulate the hierarchy of power.

The first monarchs they killed were the last ones that ever truly ruled, and The Order never faltered in their mission. In fact, they were so good at wiping out the babies that were supposed to rule that eventually, evolution caught on. The blood of the hunters that were supposed to become the new kings and queens started to go dormant, sleeping inside their blood to protect them.

Becks is a special case, seeing as how I'm technically the one responsible for waking her blood up to who she was meant to become, but that's beside the point.

Her parents did such an excellent job at living in hiding, keeping Becks safe, that The Order never even got a chance to find her and kill her while she was a baby like they'd wanted to," Absinthe said with a soft smile as his thoughts seemed to turn to the past.

"I set in motion a chain of events that even The Order wouldn't be able to penetrate, as long as Becks and her kings were kept in the dark until she made it through the gauntlet.

Yes, it led to Becks being raised in an asylum, and to all the things that happened while she was a child, but she's still alive because of what I did that day."

The guys and I shared a glance with each other, but it was Derrick who spoke next.

"How can you think that Becks is ready for the gauntlet? And you better answer now, or I swear I'll find a way around Becks' alpha order," Derrick said, unwavering in finding out what he wanted to know.

"Becks is different because of the life she's had. She hasn't been… tainted, so to speak, the way every other hunter child has. She's experienced so much already, so much that it's changed how she thinks and feels about things. It's those changes that had to be there for her to have a chance at stopping the apocalypse.

No ordinary hunter's childhood would've created the mind and heart that Becks has. And the decisions she's going to have to make? They need to be made by someone with her viewpoint of the world. No one else can make the decisions she will because no one else sees the world the same way she does.

If I'd let her stay with you guys and train in 'the ways of the hunters,' you would've ruined her… her and any chance any of us have at stopping the apocalypse. I'm sorry if that hurts to hear, but there's no better way to describe it. It's your methods that need to change to be like hers, not the other way around."

The guys and I were all shocked into silence. At least, I know I was.

He made so much sense, but everything he said went to war against every protective bone in my body.

"So, you know she's going to make it through the gauntlet then?" Adam asked, hope seeping into his voice.

I knew what he felt right then because it matched what Derrick, Tyler, and I all felt as well. We just wanted Becks to be safe because the idea of something terrible happening to her again was absolutely horrifying.

"Well, about that…," Absinthe started, and I could feel my anger coming back with a vengeance. "I can't make anyone do anything, so I can't guarantee that she's going to make it through. I was only able to give her the tools she'd need to have a chance at passing the gauntlet. I'm hoping that between her upbringing and the power I unlocked inside her, she'll do what she needs to do, but remember, guys: it's the gauntlet. There's no telling what they'll throw at her."

Absinthe's words left us all speechless again, but personally, I couldn't even begin to unpack everything he'd told us. Not yet, anyway.

With the shock of all that had happened, I suddenly realized I'd fucked my priorities up. At the top of my list should've been getting as close to Becks as I could. Not standing around, arguing with a jinn that may or may not be on our side. When, in reality, there was nothing I could do about his presence for the time being.

I shook my head as I reset the goals in my mind.

"Look, we can talk about all this later. Right now, we need to get to the stadium. Becks has already been down there for at least twenty minutes, and I can't stand not being there while she's facing whatever it is they're putting her through." Everyone seemed to agree with where my thoughts were headed, so when I said, "Tyler, take us to the gauntlet," no one put up any fuss. One by one, we each laid a hand on Tyler so he could teleport us to Hell.

I had no idea whether Becks was ready or not, but either way, there was no turning back now. She was definitely in the gauntlet, and nothing I said or did was going to change that. The best I could hope for was to put my faith in Becks and hope like hell the jinn was right.

CHAPTER 3

DERRICK

*T*he gauntlet is comprised of two parts: Hell's trials and Heaven's trials, with a twenty-four-hour intermission between them. In both realms, it takes place in a roofless stadium. Angels, demons, hunters, and the dead can all watch everything that happens while the initiate being tested fights for their life.

In the magical world, gauntlets are seen, kind of like how humans view football.

It's a major event for everyone involved.

From the dead that have nothing better to do with their eternities, to the demons and angels that like to 'claim' initiates that do really well, or fuck with those that don't, the trials have always drawn a crowd.

However, the gauntlet holds a much heavier meaning in hunter society than just some supernatural sporting event. It's quite literally life and death for one of our own. We've never taken it lightly, nor should we.

A new gauntlet has taken place almost once a week for as long as there've been hunters. Typically, an initiate's date for going to the gauntlet is known for months beforehand, if not years. Hunters related to the initiate being tested are always there, sitting front and center, so they have the best view, but they aren't the only ones who attend.

Everyone is always looking for the next 'best' initiate, bets are always placed, and no matter the initiate, there's always a decent crowd in each venue for every gauntlet.

However, as Tyler teleported us into Hell's stadium where Becks was already knee-deep in her first trial, I was shocked by how many people were already packed into the stands.

I'd probably never know how Absinthe made it happen instantly with a wave of his hand, but these hunters and demons were all here to watch Becks specifically; there was no doubt about it. Her name was on everyone's lips as they watched her in rapt excitement and cheered her on even though she couldn't hear them.

I wanted to see what was going on, but we were ushered by demons to the empty 'family' seats as soon as we landed. For that, at least, I could be grateful because it meant I was already considered her family.

I missed something while we were walking through all the hunters and demons, but the loud cheer that sounded around us left one thing for certain: Becks had done something evil, and by doing so, had won her first Hell trial, whatever that had entailed.

As we got to where we were supposed to be, I finally got my first glimpse of Becks, and the look on her face told me so much more than the blood that stained the almost translucent white room she was standing in.

Her face told me she was utterly horrified, maybe even disgusted, though I couldn't tell what'd caused her to look that way.

To us in the stands, we only get shimmering glimpses of what the initiate sees.

But to the initiate, everything seems so vividly real that quite a few initiates have never fully recovered from what they experienced in their gauntlet. As if their minds got fucked with so hard that they just weren't able to come back to the land of the living.

Like PTSD on steroids.

Becks wasn't dressed in what she was wearing when she disappeared from the beach safe house. Instead, she was wearing a blood-soaked uniform that looked like it belonged in a mental institution, and she even had the shoes to match. It didn't take me long to guess what her first trial had been about, and my heart broke for her as she turned around, faced away from us, and started running through what looked like glass.

Within the next instant, I watched her surroundings change. As her adoptive parents began to beat her, I felt such a hard pull on my chest that I nearly doubled over from the pain and shock of it.

It was Brax.

From where he hovered next to me, white-knuckling the railing in front of us with his small hands, the pain he felt was ricocheting through our connection. In that instant, I didn't know whether to be more worried about Becks or Brax.

Reaching out one of my hands to cover his, I said, "Hey. It's not real. It's just an illusion."

His sandy colored and tear-filled eyes met mine as he said, "Somebody needs to tell *her* that," and I looked back to Becks, realizing that she really had no idea what to expect here. We hadn't told her anything substantial about how the gauntlet works; we didn't want to scare her. In that moment, when it was obviously way too late to try to rectify anything, a hefty dose of guilt started seeping into my bones.

Someone landed a heavy hand on my shoulder from behind me. I turned around, planning to deck a demon if he didn't back up, but when my eyes landed on Brandt, some of the worry I felt started to ease.

Brandt, Logan, and Ben were all standing behind us as Brandt asked, "How's she doing so far? We came as soon as we heard."

"You should've called us," Logan said in my direction, disappointment with an edge of anger lacing his tone.

I glanced back over to Becks before I answered or replied to them so I could check on her, but she was still lying on a small bed of some kind, reliving what was probably one of the worst memories she had of her childhood.

Glancing back over my shoulder and raising my voice so her dads could hear me over the roar and ruckus going on around us, I said, "We just got here too. I'm pretty sure she passed her first trial, but this one doesn't look like it's going too well."

"What do you mean, you just got here? And why didn't you tell us about this the other night?" Ben asked, arms crossed over his chest as he leveled his ire at me.

Brax nearly clipped me in the face when he sent one of his hands from the rail in front of us to point to Absinthe, where he stood at the end of our group. "The jinn did this, so if you're going to be pissed at anybody, be mad at him. But either take him outside and do something about it or shut the fuck up. I'm not listening to all of you fight for the next three days."

A few seconds passed before I heard Brandt say, "I like him," with a chuckle. "I'm guessing you're Becks' familiar she was telling us about?"

Brax turned around, all of us having to avoid his big wings as he moved, and with an unprecedented amount of sarcasm, he said with false enthusiasm, "Yes, I'm Brax, Becks' familiar. You're Brandt, Logan, and Ben, Becks' dads for all intents and purposes. It's great to meet you." He turned back around with an eye roll to rival all eye rolls and said, "Now that's out of the way, can we all please, just focus already? Pixie titties!"

Laughter sounded from all her dads behind me as Logan said, "Sure thing, Boss."

Becks finally started to move again, and the look on her face sent a shiver down my spine. She was, no doubt, embracing her evil side as she stalked her adoptive parents across the space in front of us, and something in me whooped at the idea of her exacting her revenge on them, apparitions though they may have been.

Brax's gasp pulled my focus to him.

I didn't know what'd caused him to make the sound at the outset, but I knew searching his mind would be easy since he was so distracted, and I took the opportunity to see what he'd seen in his mind.

His connection with Becks might've been severed when she got here, but that didn't mean he couldn't still hear what she was thinking, and as I heard it too, through my connection with Brax, fear snaked through me as well.

Becks' power was literally talking to her, something I'd never heard of happening before. She even had a nickname for Becks!

I jerked my eyes away from Brax to watch Becks as she snatched the belt from her adoptive father, and the menacing laugh that came out of her was evil personified.

I didn't know what the implications of her power being that strong already meant or entailed. Still, as Becks started slinging the belt through the air, a foreboding uneasiness gripped me as fear for what she was capable of began to solidify in my mind.

There was no way her power should've been that strong, at least not until she got through the gauntlet completely and received the rest of her powers.

'I can't even imagine the rest of her powers if she's already this strong,' I thought as more cheers erupted throughout the stadium, and Becks won her second trial.

'I can't either,' Brax thought back at me as we all watched Becks with our mouths hanging open.

CHAPTER 4

BECKS

*A*ll the anger, bitterness, sorrow, pain, hate, and rage I felt for
my adoptive parents spilled out of me in blow after blow that
I sent flying toward their prone forms, where they quivered and
begged on the floor in front of me. Flashbacks assaulted my vision,
clouding what I saw as I released everything I felt into them, but with
each lashing I sent toward them, something in me started balking at
my behavior.

I knew it wasn't my power trying to guide me right then; that girl's
bloodlust knew no end.

No. It was *me* telling *myself* to stop.

The image of what I must've looked like flashed to the forefront of
my mind, the belt clattering to the floor as I pulled a gasp of air
through my throat.

I looked just like they had.

I was the monster now, beating on the innocent.

'Well, they're not innocent,' I heard myself think, but I shook my head

in disagreement as I found my feet stepping back and away from their huddled forms.

Suddenly, my adoptive parents started to disappear, almost like how a computer simulation will glitch first before it disappears. For a moment, I just couldn't wrap my mind around all the craziness that was going on.

However, as my surroundings began to change again, a full-on stadium taking the place of my old childhood home with me standing center stage, the final pieces of the puzzle started clicking into place in my mind.

I hadn't been in the asylum today. I hadn't actually been beating the shit out of my adoptive parents in retaliation. Absinthe's magic hadn't fucked up.

This was Hell, and I was in the gauntlet.

In no way, shape, or form had I ever imagined the gauntlet playing out like this. Honestly, I thought it was just going to be a series of pass/fail checks. Like, can you do this? Yes? Okay, next test.

There was no denying how wrong I'd been as I took in the scene around me, though.

The stadium was huge and didn't have a roof. The sky above me was a dark, burnt red color with almost black looking clouds. A roar of cheers was surrounding me, and I couldn't spot a single empty seat anywhere as I spun in a slow circle, absorbing everything I could about where I was and what was going on. There were demons and hunters and people I'd never seen before, cheering my name like they knew me, like they had some sort of stake in this game I was in, and I'd have been lying if I said a small thrill didn't trickle through my senses because of it.

The cheers started to die down as a shriek sounded through the space, causing me to whip around in the other direction.

Standing in front of a door that led into the stands, a demon stood tall in his true form.

I don't know how I knew that was what I was looking at, but as I took in his black, smoky presence, I didn't fight whatever my instincts were telling me. His eyes were glowing red, and when he snarled, black saliva spilled from his jowls, landing on the dirt floor, where the blob simmered like a smoking frying pan before the dirt literally absorbed it. The spot where the ground had pulled the saliva into itself, then opened up into some kind of hole.

I knew instantly that I couldn't fall in, or I'd die. I also knew that I'd die if I didn't find some way to defeat the demon before me. As the weight of that fell on my chest like an anchor weighing me down, I realized pretty quickly that I had no idea how to beat a demon in hand to hand combat. Call me crazy, but I'd never imagined it was something I should've been preparing for, even with the haphazard turns my life had been taking lately.

'Becksy baby, stop second-guessing yourself,' my power said in my mind. 'You know you can do anything if you have my help. Just trust me.'

I was in no position to argue with her, but trying to silence my doubts was easier said than done.

The dry dirt floor crunched beneath my feet as I took a step back. Looking down, seeing those stupid asylum shoes, I thought sarcastically, 'Well, this is not what I need to be wearing to fight a fucking demon. Why couldn't I just have my new boots, huh?'

Instantly, the asylum shoes I'd been wearing disappeared and were replaced with the very boots I'd imagined. Black lace-ups with a sturdy sole and a cushiony bottom solidified on my feet, and when I saw them, a smile played on my lips.

Apparently, my power had a lot more hidden up her sleeve than I'd ever thought possible.

Immediately, I looked back up to the demon in front of me, and as I started racing toward it, throwing caution to the wind, I knew my clothes were changing as I rushed him. Tan shorts and a black t-shirt appeared on my body as the asylum uniform melted away. As I got closer to the giant scary looking demon, I smiled as the dagger Adam had given me took shape in my hand.

"This will be easy," my power spoke through my lips, the crowd roaring even louder as if my words had been amplified for everyone to hear. However, I hadn't really done anything yet, so I didn't know what they were cheering for.

The demon bent down on all fours, dripping more of his nasty ass spit on the ground, and I just barely missed being swallowed by the hole that opened up milliseconds later.

Acting on instinct alone, I baseball slid underneath the demon between his legs as I held the dagger above me, slicing into his chest and stomach as I slid all the way out from under him on the other side. I stood quickly as he crumbled to the ground before me.

As his image started to disappear, excitement and pride flowed through me, and I jumped up, sending a fist in the air at my accomplishment.

"Good job, Becks! Keep it up!" I heard Brax's voice scream from behind me, and I whipped around to see him, the rest of my team, Absinthe, and my dads, all staring down at me with mixed emotions painted across their features.

A smile I couldn't help but wear was plastered on my face as I took them all in and watched as three more men descended the stairs, each of them messing with Derrick in some way when they got to my team's small group. One of them ruffled Derrick's dark hair, another slapped him on his shoulder, and the third came up behind him, wrapping his arms around him tightly, lifting his big frame from the ground for a second before he put him back down.

I knew they had to be Derrick's dads, and the fact that they showed up to my gauntlet without even really knowing me did some funny things in my heart place.

"You've got this, kid!" Logan screamed down at me, and as I took in the prideful look on his face, a warm feeling spread through me.

'Take a good look at them, Becksy,' my power whispered in my head. 'Look at all of them, and remember them.'

'What do you mean, remember them?' Fear laced my tone as I questioned my power.

'They are who you are fighting to save in this life, who you need to win for. Forget about the apocalypse and your past for right now. Those guys up there are all that matters. If you do what needs to be done to keep them safe, everything else will fall into place.'

The importance of what she was saying wasn't lost on me, and as I backed up, instinctively knowing another test was about to begin, I did as she told me, noting every detail I could find on each of the men and my familiar in the stands.

I would do whatever it took to make sure this wasn't the last time I saw them, to see them live for as long as possible. I didn't care how many demons I had to fight or how many memories I had to over-come and get past.

They were going to live through everything we were up against now, and whatever else life had in store for us, if I had anything to do with it. But to make that happen, I had to ensure I lived through this fucking gauntlet, so as I turned around and everything started to change again, a new kind of resolve I'd never felt in my life became my sole focus.

I could forget about myself easily, but I couldn't fail them.

As if the thoughts racing through my head about my teammates sparked some bright idea in the demons that were running this shit-show, all of a sudden, there they were before me.

Derrick, Tyler, Adam, and even Absinthe were shirtless as they were shoved roughly to their knees at my feet by faceless demons who held sick looking crossbows at the backs of each of their heads.

"What are you doing?" my voice came out strong and accusatory as I looked at the hooded demons threatening the lives of my teammates. My feet wouldn't move when I told them to, and neither would my arms, as if my body was frozen while my head wasn't.

The one holding the crossbow to Adam's head never even looked up as he answered me. "Choose, Queen."

'Why is he calling me Queen? We don't know that's what I am for sure yet.'

He might as well have been speaking a different language for all the sense that statement made. "What do you mean, choose? Choose what? Lower your weapons!" I don't know what made me think they'd listen to my command, but they didn't anyway, so it didn't matter.

"Choose, Queen," the one behind Derrick said in response, making my heart rate increase even more than it already was.

What kind of test was this anyway? I knew it wasn't real, but I still couldn't figure out what they could possibly be trying to test here. Were they trying to see if I had a favorite? Were they hoping I'd choose one and then watch as they killed the other three? Or was their goal to kill the one I chose and let the others live so they could hurt me?

Well, newsflash, I didn't have a favorite. They were all my favorites.

Yes, Absinthe was new, but dammit, he fit perfectly.

The rest of them might not like it, but I didn't ask them for permission. Kind of like how no one asked for *my* permission about most of the things we'd been doing since I met them.

"Choose, Queen," Absinthe's captor said as breathing got harder to do.

"Lower your weapons right now!" I screamed at them, but they didn't budge.

I tried to call my power, get her to speak to me again, get her to help me out, but in that instant, I couldn't find my power anywhere. I couldn't feel it within me where it usually rested, and the prospect of having to fight off all four of these demons without my power seemed impossible. Even if I could get my body to do what I was telling it to, there was no way I'd be able to save them all.

Whoever I didn't save first was going to die no matter what I did, and that action, no matter how valiant it may have been, would have been a choice in and of itself.

"Choose, Queen," the demon eyeing Tyler said, and before I could take a breath, all four of them started repeating the command in unison.

"Choose, Queen. Choose, Queen. Choose, Queen," they repeated over and over again, their voices melodic and maddening.

My heart felt like it was going to explode inside my chest with how fast it was beating, and my breathing wasn't any slower. My eyes kept bouncing between each of my teammates and Absinthe as the demons' chanting got louder.

"Come on, Becks," Tyler said, his bright green eyes glowing with power as he stared at me. "You know I'm the fun one. You'll never be bored with me, I promise!"

"What?" I heard myself ask him as the whole situation just got worse.

"I'm the sweet one. You'll never have to worry about your heart breaking with me," Adam's velvety smooth voice cut off my train of thought. "Plus, I can tell the future. You'll never be caught unawares again, Becks. Pick me."

"I know you just met me, but you already know I'm the best one here," Absinthe said as if he'd already won and the rest of the guys were beneath him. "There's no contest here."

"Becks. Look at me," Derrick said, pulling my eyes to his. "I'm the one you should choose, you know this! You'll always be safe with me." His smile made my knees weak, and had some magical-vice-of-what-the-fuck not been holding me as still as a statue, I might've fallen on my face.

"Choose, Queen," the demons kept demanding, increasing how fast they were chanting it, which only expanded all the anxiety I was already feeling.

Finally, words flew from my mouth without much thought behind them; however, every syllable was absolutely true. "I will not choose between them. Call me greedy if you have to, but I want them all, and no amount of pressure from anyone, including these very believable apparitions here, will change that! If you must kill someone, kill me instead, but I will never choose. Not ever!"

I tried not to focus too much on the fact that Absinthe was somehow included in that.

Four simultaneous crossbows fired at each of my guys then, their blood spraying me and dripping onto the ground as they all fell at my feet, face down.

I knew it wasn't real. I did.

I knew they were just apparitions of my guys' dead bodies, that they weren't actually gone. Still, my heart seized inside my chest as if they were, and it felt like my entire body was squeezing in on itself as I stared at the images before me, unable to tear my gaze away from them. My body tried to pull air into my lungs, but no air came in, and no sound went out as my mouth opened.

The shock and horror of it all didn't dissipate one bit as their bodies began to disintegrate, and the stadium came back into view, the crowd losing their minds as I realized I'd apparently won that trial.

Immediately, my eyes searched the stands for the guys to see if they were still there, and as my gaze landed on each of them, relief, sweet and all-consuming, had me dropping to my knees as I breathed in the sight of all of them.

Their smiles were infectious and proud, but I felt like I'd just been put through the emotional wringer.

'Man, fuck the gauntlet and all of its head games!' I thought as anger started chasing away my relief. *'How the literal Hell did I win that one, huh? Is it really so evil and greedy to have more than one love interest that it caused me to win a Hell trial?'*

'That's exactly what they were testing,' my power spoke up out of nowhere, startling me some. *'Greed is one of the evilest traits in this world. Your greed is love-based, but that doesn't make it any less 'wrong' in their eyes.'*

'Well then, sign me up, and send me packing right to H-E-double-fuck-ing-hockey-sticks. Pun intended,' I thought back at my power as I stood up and brushed myself off. *'Where the fuck were you during all that anyway?'*

My power didn't answer me right away, but when she did, every-thing made a bit more sense, finally. *'I couldn't influence your decisions in matters of the heart. That's all on you, Becksy baby. But there's no need to worry. Your love for each of them is true and very real. If you didn't love them the way you do, there's no way you would've passed that test. You would've chosen someone, and that would've made you fail this test in Hell. You did good.'*

'Hold on,' I thought with a bit of a giggle. *'I think it's a little early to be*

using the L-word, don't you? The rest of the team and I might've had a really good night in the incubus' lair, and Absinthe might've made me feel some things I hadn't been expecting to feel, but we're not exactly ready to start riding off into the sunset on a horse built for five, I don't think.'

'Play coy all you want, Becksy, but everyone knows how you truly feel about those boys now. The cat's out of the bag, I'm afraid,' she said.

As I looked all around me, there was no denying the truth in her words based on everyone's reactions in the stands. However, as I examined my feelings about everything quickly, I realized I was more afraid of exposing my true feelings to the guys than I was fearful of anyone else finding out.

And because life is such a cruel and unrelenting bitch, I also realized I'd just shown everyone in attendance my weaknesses in one fell swoop. The fear of what someone could do with that information had the images of my guys dying in front of me playing on repeat through my mind.

CHAPTER 5

CHIEF OTTO

I've had quite a few bad days working as a hunter and even more while being the chief of Binaria West; bad days are just par for the course with our line of work.

There is always something going on, some disturbance in the balance that needs to be rectified, and usually, some price that needs to be paid to fix what went too wrong or too right.

However, the past few days had ranked right on up there as some of the worst I'd ever experienced.

It was a hard pill to swallow that Tina had turned out to be a traitor and had somehow managed to convince about a third of my hunters to agree with her way of thinking. Now I was short-staffed on an almost laughable scale while the threats to the balance had only increased ten-fold over the last few days.

The fact that little Philippa was, so far, the only hope we had at saving the entire vampire species didn't give me much hope either. I'd been watching her while Dragon team was gone. With each new team barging into my office to tell me about the next calamity that'd happened or was going to happen, Philippa had picked up on my growing anxiety. More than once, I'd had to stop her from ripping people apart in my defense.

Add to that how remarkably upsetting it was that every other species had chosen this moment in time to lose their minds, particularly the werewolves and Merpeople, while everything else was going on... I had more on my proverbial plate than I'd ever had before.

But even all that paled compared to what I felt when no one could find Dragon team, dead or alive.

I knew a lot of lives were lost during their battle with Tina and her forces, including way too many innocent fairies and pixies that had been caught in the crossfire. Of course, as luck would have it, Tina wasn't included in the death toll, and Dragon team was nowhere to be found, a combination that I didn't really know how to handle.

Blood and dirt had been traipsed all through the safe house they'd been staying in, but there was no sign of them otherwise, as if they'd just disappeared into thin air.

Yes, I might've valued Dragon team more than other teams because I knew they were the key to stopping the apocalypse, but the way my heart ached when we couldn't find them, had more to do with the fact that I loved each of them as if they were my own children than anything else.

I'd known Derrick, Adam, and Tyler their whole lives, an instinctual drive to keep a close eye on them, present in my mind from day one for each of them. I'd had that same drive the day I found out about Rebecca, too, probably even more substantially than I'd felt it for the rest of her team if I had to be painfully honest.

However, if there was one thing I'd learned from leading all of these people during my time as chief, it was that I had to trust my teams, no matter how hard that particular aspect of my job might've been since Tina decided to get her revenge in the worst possible way.

I couldn't 'helicopter parent' the teams I led despite how much I wished I could. My job required me to stay at a distance, monitoring, advising, and planning out my teams' next moves so they could all have the best possible outcome. Most of the time, no good could come from me following them around to ensure they stayed safe.

Nevertheless, when Silkie team busted into my office while I was trying unsuccessfully to keep Philippa distracted, telling me that Rebecca was already in her gauntlet, no amount of reasoning with myself could win over my need to protect her.

I was livid.

I wanted to dole out justice by force and ask questions later. I wanted to stop what was happening, pull Rebecca to me, and keep her safe from the life I knew she was going to have to live, but there was no getting around what had already happened, no avoiding what already seemed to have been written in stone.

Rebecca was in Hell somehow, and the only thing I could do about it was go down there, watch her trials, and try my damnedest to advise her as best I could between the tests she was going to face, while at the same time, trying to keep the world from ending in the process.

However, when Philippa jumped up on my back and refused to let go, murmuring unintelligible but encouraging sounds in my ear, I had to stop myself.

I didn't have anyone else I trusted to leave her with, no one here at least. At this point, I really only trusted Dragon team, given everything that had happened with Tina and the number of hunters who'd also proven to be traitorous.

'I can't take her with me, right?' I asked myself as my mind worked fast to find a solution, but right after that thought rolled through my mind, Philippa stilled on my back, causing me to turn my head so I could see her face.

There was a remarkable amount of understanding in those big eyes of hers, and when she nodded her head at me as if she knew exactly what I'd been thinking, there was little doubt in my mind that I could, in fact, take her with me to Hell.

'She is technically dead,' I thought as I stared at her in wonder, a

brand new set of possibilities wandering about my mind as I weighed my options.

Eventually, though, I decided there wouldn't be any harm done to her if we were wrong; we just wouldn't be allowed to pass from this realm to Hell's. If that turned out to be the case, I was prepared to find another option, but my worries started to ease some as we passed through without difficulty.

~

"Alright, Dragon team, give me her stats," I said above the roar of the crowd as Philippa and I came back into existence behind Rebecca's team. I noticed a second or two later that Derrick's fathers were present, as were Rebecca's parents' teammates, and even though I wanted to greet each of them, shake their hands, and catch up with them, I had to know what was going on first.

Brax's eyes got hilariously larger than normal as he saw Philippa clinging to my back. "You brought Philippa down here?!" he choked out in a voice that sounded equal parts mortified and intrigued. "How...?" his question died off as Philippa jumped from my back, nearly knocking him over as she landed in his arms with a surprising amount of finesse.

"We can figure out how she was able to come here later," I said with a small chuckle as Philippa's antics made a smile form on my face. "I figured you guys and Rebecca wouldn't want me leaving her with just anyone after what you've all been through."

Tyler and Adam nodded at my statement but quickly turned their attention back to Rebecca, where she watched her teammates and some other man being shoved to their knees before her. Derrick looked put out, which was a common occurrence with him whenever I decided something he didn't particularly agree with. I could tell he didn't think bringing the vampire child to Hell was the right move, but after a second, I could also tell when he realized I didn't have any other option. Everything played across his features as if I were reading a book of his thoughts, and soon enough, he was telling me what I needed to know without an argument.

"This is her fourth Hell trial," he began as I heard the demons in front of Rebecca tell her to choose between the men at her feet. However, when they called her 'Queen,' a hush began to fill the entire stadium, cutting off Derrick's words as well, as we all watched what was about to happen.

'So, she is *destined to be the next queen?'* I thought with a smile I couldn't get rid of.

So far, all I'd been able to do was speculate about what she would become, but as the demons continued to call her that, every question in my mind about Rebecca's possible role in the future died away. And good riddance to those thoughts too. They'd been plaguing me from the moment Brax busted into my office and told me about her in the first place.

Rebecca's unorthodox upbringing didn't just happen sponta-neously. It shouldn't have happened at all. Whenever things that unor-dinary transpired, I always had to pay very close attention to them because it usually meant something significant. And in Rebecca's case, since she was obviously destined to become the next queen, every-thing made more sense than it ever had before. The demons never would've called her that if they didn't already see her that way.

A plethora of tasks started weaving their way through my mind, one right after another, in an almost bottomless list of what we were going to have to do as soon as Rebecca made it through the gauntlet, tasks that I found myself excited to see come to fruition. Ensuring she received the rest of her powers, making sure she chose and bound herself to whoever her kings were going to be, setting up the cere-mony to name her queen in front of all the hunters, both from here and from Binaria East, restructuring the entire hunter organization... I was definitely going to be busy over the next few months, if not years, if I could get her to keep me on as one of her advisors or something.

Those were all things I would be more than happy to plan out and facilitate, as long as she made it through her gauntlet, that was.

Destiny or not, nothing could make her pass the gauntlet if her soul wasn't balanced enough for the job. However, if she did make it through, many things would have to change from how they were being done now.

Yes, it might mean I'd be out of my job leading Binaria West, but I couldn't care less about that if it meant things could go back to the way they were when the kings and queens reigned. From what I knew, that time was marked by far fewer disturbances in the balance and far more happiness in all the creatures and realms.

I'd tried my hardest to handle what was thrown at me, to get the balance back to the way it had been back then, but as the demons started chanting "Choose, Queen," over and over again, I knew the hunters were never meant to be run this way.

The hunters needed their monarchs, and Rebecca was who needed to be at the helm, guiding us out of our misguided ways.

When Rebecca said she'd never choose between them, I knew she'd won that trial; there was no denying it. As I watched her drop to her knees, an intensely emotional look of relief on her face as she caught sight of her teammates where they stood before me, I had a pretty strong hunch about who she would choose to have as her kings.

However, as I looked at the guy standing at the end of the row beside Adam and realization started to seep into my senses, an almost overwhelming punch of anger and rage went right to my gut.

"Absinthe," I said, unable to control how much emotion could be heard in that one word. "What are you doing here?"

Derrick's and Rebecca's fathers all shifted their focus to look at the jinn in front of us as they heard the name, as did all of Dragon team, including Brax.

I couldn't let that go unnoticed, so I let it strengthen me since I wasn't the only one upset by his presence. Then the image of the four men on their knees before Rebecca flashed through my mind, and I had to fight against the drive I felt to try and kill the jinn right then, even with how useless it would've been since he's immortal.

How could he have possibly been included in Rebecca's gauntlet? Why wouldn't she have killed him in that trial, given the fact that it would've probably saved the rest of her team? Did she know who he was, what he was capable of?

"Hello, Chief," Absinthe said as he turned around and bowed his head respectfully in my direction. "I know you must have a lot of questions for me."

"I certainly do," I responded angrily. "What is the meaning of all this?" My hands gestured to encompass everything that no longer made as much sense as I thought it had only moments before.

Philippa caught my attention as I noticed she'd let go of Brax, climbed across the unoccupied seats in front of me, and started making her way hesitantly in Absinthe's direction. Something told me she'd be fine. Something else told me I needed to protect her as well, but I didn't get a chance to respond before Absinthe was speaking directly to Philippa.

"Philippa," he said in a tone that threw me off for how reverently he said it. "I've been waiting a long time to finally meet you. Come," he said as he opened his arms for her to climb up onto him. She did so without hesitating, and he spoke to her as if he was almost afraid of disappointing her. "I will answer questions for you too, and I will fix whatever I can, but we're going to have to wait until Becks is through with her Hell trials. Is that okay? I really don't want to miss the last three here."

Again, with that surprising amount of understanding in her eyes, Philippa nodded at him and seemed to settle in his arms as she turned her excited gaze to Rebecca, where she was looking about the area sporadically. Nothing else had appeared to us in the stands yet, so it was impossible to tell what she was seeing or experiencing.

"I need answers now," I said as I crossed my arms over my chest, unwilling to let Absinthe hold Philippa or be involved with Rebecca unless it was proven to me that he wasn't a danger to either of them. All the dads around me nodded their agreement with my words, and something about them having my back fueled my resolve.

Brax looked like he was about to explode from all the stress he was feeling, but he did his best to explain what had happened while they were gone. His voice was angry and dripped with a level of sarcasm I didn't think he was able to avoid.

"We were all incapacitated in our fight with Tina and her minions, and to save our lives, Becks made a dumbass deal with Absinthe. It saved our lives, but that's the only good I've seen come of it since. I don't know why Becks didn't just let us die, but she didn't, and now, here we are. She also gave all of us an alpha order not to try and kill him," Brax said that last part on a hiss as he eyed the jinn. "That's the only reason he still breathes."

"We're not under any alpha order," Brandt said as he cracked his knuckles and motioned to the rest of Essence team beside me, his Viking heritage unmistakable in both his stature and demeanor. "You just say the word, Brax, and we'll handle him, no problem."

"We'll help," the retired members of Raven team said, almost in unison, but as much as I would've liked to have Absinthe locked back up for the rest of eternity based on what I thought I knew about him, I quickly realized, I really didn't know everything. I certainly didn't know what Rebecca's reasoning was for relying on the jinn's help when she had so many other options available to her.

However, the fact that she'd had him included in her trial, right there beside Derrick, Adam, and Tyler, spoke volumes. I couldn't ignore that.

Whatever role Absinthe had to play might've still been up in the air, but the fact that he did have a part to play was undeniable.

"Hold off for now," I said, quieting and stilling the men surrounding me. "I want to talk to Rebecca before we make any moves that could jeopardize the future."

Each of the men around me looked in my direction as if I'd lost my mind but backed off anyway, even though I could tell it was hard for them.

"Alright, Boss," I heard someone say behind me, but I'd already been distracted by Rebecca too much to pay attention to who'd said it.

She was crawling on the ground as her new environment started to shimmer into existence. Within a matter of moments, her usually healthy-looking frame took on a sickening hue, and her body had to have lost at least thirty pounds - thirty pounds I don't think she had to lose in the first place. Her cheeks were sunken, her hair was frazzled about everywhere, and even from this distance, I could see her lips were so dry they were cracked beyond recognition.

'What the hell is this? I've never seen a trial like this before, ever.'

CHAPTER 6

BECKS

I fucking hate being hungry.

When you're feeling snacky, the small pangs are bad enough, but the kind of hunger that seems like it will rip you apart from the inside out? The kind where you're so hungry that you almost aren't anymore, as if your body has just given up on the idea entirely, all while it literally starts eating everything inside you that it can get its greedy ass hands on?

Well, I wished that fate on no one. Not even Rick, and I still hated that motherfucker with a passion so strong, I'd kill him again if I was ever given a chance without batting an eye.

One minute I was fine, though emotionally drained from seeing my guys murdered, and I knew for sure that I was in the gauntlet. The next minute, my reality was so consumed with what I was experiencing, the trials were nearly forgotten.

I was in the sparsest, most arid desert I could've ever imagined.

Then came 'the suck' as I would forever remember it.

I could feel my body being drained of everything that was keeping it alive. The same fat I'd seen in the mirror and sneered at left my body in a swirl of red smoke that surrounded me, and in that moment, I was begging for it to come back. Fuck how it made me look so long as it kept me alive.

My throat felt like the cells that made it were literally nothing more than shriveled up masses of uselessness with how thirsty I was. As I fell to the ground again, fighting to stay conscious and alive, a gasp tore through my dry windpipe with a shot of pain so intense it felt like razors dragging along my esophagus.

Dazed, my vision blurring, I tried to find some way to relieve everything I was feeling. I looked around, but there was nothing as far as I could see, but more and more desert, the sun beating down against me as if it had a personal vendetta against my body.

I think I lost consciousness there for a second or two, but as my vision started to clear just enough for me to make out my surroundings, a building appeared in front of me.

It was a log cabin that was in no way there only moments before, but somehow, there it was, and I was lying on the ground right at the foot of the steps that led up to its porch.

Getting up onto my hands and knees, I crawled over to the steps and started climbing them on all fours, only barely able to make it to my feet once I was all the way out of the sun's rays. It was at least twenty degrees cooler in the shade of the porch's overhanging roof, and even though breathing and standing, and just living in the first place was still an exhaustive task, it was still a hell of a lot better than being out in the baking sun.

I forced my legs to carry me over to the door, but as I raised my hand to knock because that was the only thing I could think to do at the time, the door swung open, and a man that looked to be in the same terrible state that I was, stood before me.

"Are you who I've been waiting for?" the man asked, his voice coming out sounding like he hadn't spoken in a while as his face scrunched up like it hurt him to speak.

I had no idea what he was talking about, so I answered in the only way I knew how.

"What?" I asked him, my voice sounding just as bad as his did.

He sighed a little, as his entire body slumped. "I'll take that as a no," he said as he turned around and motioned for me to follow him inside.

Seeing as how there weren't any other options, I followed him, noting his sunken skin and slow gait. His beard was long and untrimmed, his hair a wiry nest of fly-aways that fell from his head in every direction.

"Come on in; we'll wait in this hellhole together."

I shut the door behind me but stood with my back against it because I didn't know what to expect. Plus, the prospect of moving even an inch further seemed like more than my body was capable of.

Looking around, I noticed there was nothing here. Like literally nothing in the cabin. Just four walls, the door I was pressed up against, creaky and dangerous-looking floorboards, and two windows; that was it.

The man went to the far wall and leaned up against it, mirroring my stance across the cabin from me, before he sighed a heavy breath and asked, "You didn't see anything on your way here, did you?"

"What do you mean?" I asked, having almost forgotten how I'd gotten here in the first place.

"Have you seen any animals, any streams, anything?" he asked, apparently getting upset with my inability to understand what he meant the first time.

I was having a tough time trying to remember anything but the scorching sun and the endless hunger I felt, so I just shook my head in response, hoping that would suffice.

"Figures," the guy said. "I've been here for a year, and there's been nothing but this place the whole time…" he paused for a breath, seeming to think a sudden thought. "Well, until you came."

His entire demeanor changed then. His head tilted downward some, his eyes narrowed in on me, and his stance seemed to get more determined as he leaned forward a little and sent his hands out in front of him.

I couldn't help but feel like this man was eyeing me up to be his next meal literally, and with as bad as I was already feeling, I couldn't even begin to imagine fighting him off.

'Fucking seriously?' I asked in my head, but no one answered, and for the life of me, I couldn't understand why I thought someone would.

The man started creeping toward me, his left leg trailing behind him some, so his body was angled on his approach.

My brain was a mixture of two resounding thoughts. One, to just let him kill me because at this point, having someone bite into me seemed like a sweet release from the pain I was feeling. And two, to find whatever energy I was using to stay upright and use it to fight him off, possibly even resorting to cannibalism if it came to it.

However, I quickly dismissed both ideas as a glass of water, and a plate with a single piece of bread appeared out of nowhere on the floor between us.

The man fell to his knees and immediately started crying as he eyed the sustenance, crawling over to it as if... well, as if it were the lifeline he'd needed.

However, my reaction to seeing it wasn't much better. I didn't drop to my knees, but tears did form in my eyes, and my feet started moving without me telling them to move. "We should share it, then try to come up with another way to get out of here," I said to the man as we both got closer to the bread and water.

But upon hearing my words, he stopped moving and sent a glare my way that told me under no uncertain terms, he would not be sharing that with me under any circumstance.

'But dude has been here for a year! If he takes all of that, who knows how long I'll have to feel this way,' I thought as I eyed the man with a glare of my own.

"I've been here longer, so it's mine."

He barely finished his sentence before he was dashing toward the bread and water, and I didn't hesitate to try and get to it before he did. I threw everything I had into getting there first, but he still beat me to it.

He picked up the glass almost reverently and brought it up to his lips gently before tilting it back and slowly letting the liquid slide into his mouth.

Still on his knees, I had an advantage because I was still standing, and when he'd drank about half of the glass, I reached out and swiped it out of his hand quickly, sending it to my lips instantly.

I swallowed the life-giving liquid as fast as I could, but I didn't get more than two large gulps down before the guy was football tackling me to the ground, the water dropping from my hands and spilling all across the floor in the process.

"What the fuck?" I yelled as the man started swinging his fists wildly in my direction, landing crazed blows everywhere he could.

I threw my hands up to protect my face, but the motion was useless since he didn't seem to care about where he hit me, so long as he was hitting me, period.

By the time I got my wits about me, I was almost convinced that it was too little too late. He'd wrapped both of his big hands around my throat and had already started squeezing as a small dose of clarity came to my mind.

I didn't know what told me to imagine tearing him apart, but once I did, once I saw his body in my mind, ripped to shreds, something of a purple-ish blue color burst out of me like a sunburst, slicing through the man where he sat on top of me.

Hot blood and chunks of flesh coated everything, including me, but my hunger didn't care. Not one bit. It was as if I was possessed as I crawled up onto my hands and knees and started making my way over to the plate that still sat in the center of the room.

My eyes focused in on the blood-soaked piece of bread, and everything else disappeared from existence, almost like when you stare in a single spot for too long, everything else in your field of vision starts to darken.

That bread was my ticket to life, and though I might not have been able to recall exactly why I wanted to live right then, I knew for sure that I did.

I picked it up and thrust the entire piece of bread into my mouth without even taking the time to bite it like a normal, civilized human being would. It tasted like the sweetest heaven, and my eyes rolled to the back of my head as I savored it, slick saliva finally starting to coat my mouth for the first time in what felt like forever.

Suddenly, I was on the dirt floor of the stadium again, and the whiplash of realities that I'd been thrust through was so disorienting that it probably took me a solid minute to figure out what the fuck was going on.

The crowd was roaring louder than I'd heard them before, chanting something I couldn't quite comprehend. But as I realized I was still on my knees with blood dripping from me everywhere, I stood up quickly, reveling in the fact that I felt like myself again, and tried to seem somewhat dignified despite what I must have looked like during that trial.

"Quinque! Quinque! Quinque!" I finally made out what the crowd was saying, but I still had no idea what they meant by the word.

I turned in a slow circle, taking everything and everyone in, and though I could tell I was doing good by the way the crowd was acting, I'd have been lying if I said I didn't feel terrible about what I'd done to earn their approval.

That guy had died. He'd died a horrible, bloody death after starving for a year. *'How is that even possible?'* I wondered, but I was in Hell, so I guessed it didn't have to make sense. The point still remained.

I was selfish, and I was evil.

BEFORE I COULD REALLY EVEN GET my bearings and wrap my mind around everything that had happened, another man stood before me.

The sight of him took my breath away.

He was the epitome of what I would call the perfect man, jaw-droppingly handsome on a level my brain almost short-circuited looking at, and when his light blue eyes lighted on mine, my mouth opened, but no sound came out. His skin was a dark tan, almost caramel in color, and his black hair shined in the light that was left in the red sky above us.

I couldn't look away from him. Not at all.

"Hello, Queen Rebecca," he said in a voice that sent shivers up my spine and had tingles erupting everywhere under my skin. "I'm Asmodeus, the original demon of lust."

"Uh-huh," I said with the intellectual response of a fucking rock. "I can see that."

His smile was out of this world gorgeous. Well... we weren't on Earth, but the sentiment stood regardless.

"I'm here to present your last two tests," he said, but I barely heard him over the sound of my own heart beating. "You should feel special. I only lead the best of the best through their trials."

I couldn't even begin to unpack whatever the fuck he meant by that, much less form a coherent thought once he reached out and slid his hand into mine, leading me on a leisurely stroll across the packed dirt beneath us.

"Your sixth test is a simple one with only two options, and is probably one of my favorites to administer."

"Uh-huh," I said again, slapping myself mentally for not being able to speak like I had any sense as I continued to stare up at him, even though I probably should've been looking where I was going.

"As you know, Tina has caused many problems on Earth, as well as in the Veil. Those actions have had far-reaching consequences that have touched us all the way down here, in my home. I don't take very kindly to such things, such nuisances. In fact, I dislike the disruptions she's caused so much, I'm willing to use the powers I have to change the course of history. Since you have fought her first-hand, I designed this test so that we could both get what we want out of it. You get to win a trial, and I get to have my peace back."

"What's the test?" I heard myself ask, and I knew my power was finally starting to wake up and help me again.

"It's simple," he said as he let go of my hand and took a few steps back, creating about a four-foot distance between us.

A crib appeared with a snap of his fingers, and inside, a baby was sleeping soundly. It was wrapped in pink blankets, and its hands were balled into tight little fists that laid limply near its head. I stared down at the child, unaware of how I was able to tear my gaze away from the demon of lust before me, but didn't question it.

"This is Tina," Asmodeus said, causing my gaze to shoot back up to his.

He was smirking a sinfully sexy half-smile at me, a hint of danger evident behind his unreal looking eyes, and I knew instantly I wasn't going to like what he was about to say.

"If you could go back in time and eliminate her from ever being a threat to anyone, would you?" He didn't pause to give me a chance to answer before he was speaking again. "Well, this is your lucky day, Queen Rebecca. All you have to do is kill her now, and you will rewrite the course of history. You will take her and all of the decisions she ever made out of existence.

Kill her now, and everything will go back to how it was supposed to be. Or don't, and live with the fact that you could've prevented everything that's happening for the rest of your life."

My mouth dropped open as I looked at him, but again, no sound came out, stunned as I was by what he'd said.

I couldn't kill a baby! No fucking way. Even if that baby was going to grow up and try to end the entire world by starting an apocalypse. Even if that baby was going to end up being the reason I inevitably ended up living the life I'd lived so far.

I might not have agreed with Tina and the things she'd done, but her story still floated through my mind as Asmodeus waited for me to answer him.

She'd been the victim of a horrible crime, losing her entire family in the process. It made her hate humanity and caused her to have a score to settle with God himself. Call me crazy, but I understood her pain, the reason behind all of her actions. In her own sick and twisted way, I knew she actually thought she was helping everyone by ending everything, by starting an apocalypse that wiped everyone out. No one could feel the pain she had felt if they didn't exist.

Did that mean she was a bad person?

Probably, but it was her trauma that made her that way, and that was a fact I couldn't just ignore. I couldn't act as if it didn't play a critical role in how everything went down.

Not to mention I wasn't looking at the version of Tina who'd already made all those bad decisions. I was looking at the version of her from before she'd ever done anything wrong. The baby in front of me was innocent. No one is born evil, right?

Now, if he'd presented me with the guy who'd killed Tina's family in the first place, I might have had to reconsider, but he didn't, even though that would've made a lot more sense, at least in my opinion.

"I can't do it," I said resolutely, my voice coming out stronger and more confident than I felt.

I knew it was going to disappoint the demon before me, and for a moment, I questioned why that bothered me at all, but as his face got stern, he nodded in response.

No one was cheering anymore, and I knew that couldn't have been a good sign, but I had to stick with what made the most sense to me, and dammit, I wasn't killing an innocent on purpose if I had anything to say about it.

Yes, I'd killed innocents during these trials, but I did take some solace in the fact that it wasn't real, that they were simply apparitions. At least, they were, for the most part.

I was pretty sure that the baby version of Tina was real; however, I'd probably never be able to prove that hunch.

As soon as the demon nodded his head, the crib disappeared, and rather than looking upset for longer than a few seconds, Asmodeus had another smile forming on his lips when he reached out to retake my hand.

"On to your last test, Queen Rebecca."

CHAPTER 7

BECKS

*A*smodeus led me a few steps away from where the crib had been, and unintentionally, I think, had me facing my team-mates in the stands. I was too far away to really read their faces, but I didn't have time to try and analyze them anyway.

The lust demon beside me captured my attention as he said, "Again, this will be a simple trial. You only have to choose between two possible outcomes."

Instantly, I was thrust into another reality, and I fought as hard as I could to remember that it was just a vision, that I wasn't actually there. Going through all these trials was bad enough, but losing myself to them like I had before, only added a whole other layer of suffering I wanted to avoid by any means necessary.

Perspective and the lens through which we view the world are everything, and I didn't want to have my viewpoint fucked with if I could help it.

I was standing in the corner of a small living room, next to the front door. There wasn't much to look at, and everything in the space was a bit dated. Still, it seemed pretty homey anyway, even though there weren't any pictures on the walls to add to the place's overall feel.

A hand landed lightly on my shoulder, and as I looked up, I saw Asmodeus again, staring down at me with a look I couldn't quite place, settled handsomely on his face.

"Here, you only need to watch. No one can see or hear you, so there's no use in wasting your breath. Simply watch and absorb," he said, and though I wanted to ask a million questions of him, I ignored that desire and nodded as my real parents walked into the room from a doorway that I assumed led to the kitchen.

I knew the demon told me they couldn't hear or see me, but I tried to move closer to them anyway, only to find that yet again, my body wouldn't do what I was telling it to. I was frozen as I watched my parents come into the living room and sit down on the couch with light smiles on their faces. It was infuriating that I couldn't interact with them. Still, as the vision continued, I found myself listening intently, trying to do exactly as Asmodeus had said and absorb everything I could.

Suddenly, the door at my back swung open, and Brandt, Logan, and Ben busted in through the door and through me as if I were a ghost, startling an adorable squeak out of my mother, who, upon seeing them, jumped up and ran to them.

Their arms engulfed her as her ecstatic laugh sounded through the space. "What are you guys doing back here?" she asked before Logan picked her up and spun her around in a circle a couple of times.

"We have some news," Brandt said, his tone unmistakably happy.

Logan put my mother down, and her eyes landed on Brandt with worry written all across her face. "What is it?" she asked, her voice full of trepidation.

Brandt smiled down at her. "You know, good things can happen to hunters, too, right?"

My mom's face turned bright red as her smile spread, but she didn't say anything more before Ben explained, "Tina has been handled, and all the tethers to the Void that were opened up are closed again!"

"What?" my mother asked, reminding me of myself in an almost disturbing kind of way. "How's that possible? What happened?"

Ben walked over to my mother smoothly, standing tall as he looked down into her eyes lovingly. "Does it matter? The last few weeks don't have to be the last we spend with each other. We can be together again." His hand went out to cup my mother's cheek, and the look on her face told me that nothing else mattered to her at all in that moment.

"I guess not," she said on a breathy giggle, her eyes locked on Ben's.

Without a warning of any kind, a gray blur tumbled out of thin air, barreling between my mom and the rest of Essence team, hitting Brandt and Malcolm as it passed them by and landed in a pile of stone and bat wings on the floor near where I was standing.

Brax stood up shakily, dusting himself off with his back turned to the group behind him, where they were all poised and ready to attack, forming a wall to block my mother behind them.

"Pixie titties and fairy farts! Those angels couldn't give a 'goyle a little more warning before they just throw me from Heaven? Ugh," he said as his familiar anger made a smile spread on my face.

Turning around, he stood with his hands on his hips and looked at each of the members of Essence team, where they looked down on him, obviously demanding answers with their expressions alone.

"I'm Brax."

"What are you doing here?" Malcolm asked, a dagger I hadn't seen him with before, gripped tightly in his hand.

Brax sighed and lifted himself up into the air. He was a little wobbly on his wings, but he righted himself quickly enough. "I need to speak with Amanda Woodridge."

Everyone visibly tensed, but my mother stepped between all of her guys without an ounce of hesitation, her chin held high as she regarded my familiar. "Call me Mandy. What do you need to speak with me about?"

Brax nodded at my mother, but looked a little concerned as he asked, "Are you sure you want them to hear what I have to say? It's kind of a private matter."

As could be guessed, each of the guys on my mom's team sneered at that, and Brandt said the most stereotypical thing he could've said in that moment. "Anything you need to say to her, you can say in front of us."

My mother had her back to her guys as she rolled her eyes with a smile on her face.

'I knew I'd like her,' I thought as she said, "It's fine. What do you need to say?"

Brax shrugged but answered her anyway. "I'm your child's familiar."

The room went deathly silent, and I didn't think anyone was actually breathing for a solid minute. Eventually, my mother asked, her voice a little shaky, "What child?"

Brax smiled at her and nodded toward her stomach, and instantly, my mother's hands went to rest on the lowest part of her abdomen, a single tear welling up in one of her eyes to drop down her face silently.

"I'm pregnant?" she asked, almost to herself right before her guys erupted into elated hysterics, swinging her around, hugging her, slapping each other on the back in good-natured happiness.

Brax's smile was infectious, and Essence team's jovial excitement had a smile so wide on my face that my cheeks hurt.

"I'll just give you guys some time to process," Brax said as he turned around and started heading my way, presumably so he could walk through the door behind me, but my mother grabbed his arm before he could make it more than a foot away from them.

"Wait," she said. "How do you know this? Who are you?"

Brax turned back around, saying, "I'm Brax, your new daughter's familiar. Her heart just started beating when the angels assigned me to her, and they immediately sent me here to tell you."

"It's a girl?" Logan asked, but my mother didn't seem to care about that as much as he did.

"She's going to need a familiar?" my mother asked, her face full of concern and worry over a child she just found out about, and instantly, I loved her more for it.

Brax smiled and placed his hands on his hips as he stood up proudly. "Yes, she's going to have a life where she'll need me, but I will do everything in my power to protect her and keep her safe, to keep her on the right path, and to see that she has the best life she can possibly have."

He was so adorable when he said things like that, and a small giggle escaped my mother and me at the same time as we watched him.

Within the next instant, things started to get blurry, and it took me a second to wrap my mind around what I'd just witnessed as the scene started changing before me.

Brax had told me that when he showed up to tell my parents about me, they'd been on the run. However, the rest of their team hadn't made it into his version of the story.

He'd said Malcolm and Mandy were living off the grid in a small house in Arizona at the time, which seemed to check out.

Even though that part of Brax's story seemed legit, the fact that he left out all of Essence team being there, that they thought everything was going to turn out alright, that they thought Tina had been taken care of, all seemed like some pretty extensive details to have left out.

I also remembered the looks on the living members of Essence team as I told them I was Malcolm and Mandy's daughter the other night.

If they'd been present when she found out she was pregnant with me, the genuine reactions I'd seen in the incubus lair had to have been fraudulent.

But that didn't make any sense to me.

However, when the new scene completely solidified in front of me, I didn't doubt the story Brax had told me anymore because I knew what I was seeing was a lie.

My mother and the rest of her team were all posted up around a swing set where a younger version of me swung on a swing with three boys that looked to be around the same age as I appeared to be.

I knew what I looked like at around nine years old, seeing how the asylum ensured I had a picture taken of me every year. However, when I was nine, I was in the asylum. I wasn't swinging on a swing with the childhood versions of Derrick, Adam, and Tyler.

I looked up to see Asmodeus smiling down at me.

"What is all this?" I asked him as I turned my attention back to the scene I was supposed to be watching.

The younger version of Adam planted a kiss on my nine-year-old cheek quickly before he dashed off toward the slide, the younger versions of Derrick and Tyler chasing after him, yelling something about it not being his turn.

The reaction from Brandt had been hilarious, too, since his large frame bucked as he stepped in front of my younger self, yelling at Adam to keep his hands and lips to himself.

"This is what your life could've been like had a few key things never happened," Asmodeus said, causing me to look back up at him.

"What do you mean?"

"I mean, this is what your life should've been," he said as he gestured before him, and the scenes started fading in and out quickly but playing in slow motion while I watched them.

The park scene flew away while another took its place, slowing down so I could see it clearly before it too was swiped away.

In that one, I was probably around twelve years old, and my mother was putting makeup on me. I don't know how I knew it was the first time I was wearing makeup or that she'd spent an hour trying to get the tangled mass of my brown hair to cooperate, but I did. I also knew somehow that she was getting me ready for a dance of some kind and that I was incredibly nervous.

"I love this, Mama, but what if the guys hate me when they see me this way? They're probably going to laugh their heads off at me," I said in the vision, nearly succumbing to the tears that wanted to well up in my eyes.

My mother stopped what she was doing to kneel down in front of me, taking my hands in hers. "Those boys have loved you from the moment they first laid eyes on you, Becksy. I promise, they're not going to know what to do with themselves when they look at you tonight."

Little me nodded but looked down at my knees anyway.

My mother wasn't having that, though.

Lifting my chin with a delicate finger, she brought my eyes to hers again as she asked, "Do *you* feel pretty right now?"

It took a second, but I saw myself nod toward her in response.

"Then that's all that matters. You don't need those boys' approval to feel good, theirs or anyone else's. You are beautiful inside and out, Becksy, and the sooner you truly know that in here," she said as she pressed her hand to my heart, "the sooner all those crazy feelings you're feeling will start to go away."

Tears were welling up inside my eyes as the scene changed again quickly, and I wiped my eyes discreetly, hoping no one saw how much that one had affected me.

The next one was really just a flash of me where I looked to be around fifteen, lying on a couch, surrounded by Brandt, Logan, Malcolm, and Ben with a big bucket of popcorn in each of our laps as we all watched something on tv.

Something happened in the movie that made me jump like mad and caused me to spill popcorn all over myself and the couch. However, instead of getting angry or something... hell, I don't know what I'd expected... but instead of anything like that, Brandt picked up a few pieces of popcorn that had rolled over to him and threw them at me. And rather than flinch or something, the other version of me opened her mouth and caught the pieces out of thin air as if it were a game they'd played numerous times before.

Ben, Malcolm, and Logan shared a mischievous grin before they gathered all the popcorn around them and started chucking them at me at the same time.

"I can't catch them all when you throw them that fast, guys!" I heard myself laugh as I watched myself get bombarded with popcorn, as they not only threw what was laying around them, but what was in their buckets as well.

My mother walked in then, and smiling, she said, "Y'all are cleaning all of that up, do you hear me?"

I watched as all of them looked at each other sheepishly for a second before simultaneously, they all started throwing popcorn at my mother. She started laughing as she tried to dodge the popcorn bullets, but seeing it was a useless endeavor, she then decided to run and jump on younger me, tickling me like a madwoman as the whole room descended into bouts of laughter.

The scene swooshed away too quickly, and in the next instant, I saw myself, dressed in a white gown under a starry night sky, walking toward a wide aisle with Brandt holding my right arm, Logan holding my left, while Malcolm and Ben walked on the other sides of Brandt and Logan.

Derrick, Adam, and Tyler stood at the other end of the aisle, and as soon as I saw them, the scene shifted again... and again, and again, each vision more heart wrenching than the last.

By the time it was over, I was quietly crying so hard it was hard to comprehend much beyond my emotions, but when Asmodeus spoke next, my breath hitched in my throat.

"Your choice is easy. Choose to keep the life you've had so far, or choose the one you just witnessed."

"What?" I asked while the memory of my mother asking that same question, in the same way I usually did, flashed through my mind quickly.

Asmodeus' lips formed a thin line before he said, "Choose, Queen Rebecca." He paused for a split second. "Well, if you choose to have the life I showed you, you will no longer be queen, but I hardly think that matters to you."

A half-hearted chuckle escaped my throat at that, but as the memories played through my mind, I realized there was no choice here. The life he showed me was what I'd always wanted - a normal one, with a family that actually loved me.

Those visions had been the most beautiful things I'd ever experienced, and yet, they weren't even real.

"If I choose what you showed me, will it actually happen? Or is this just a regular trial, where no matter what I choose, the past won't change?"

Asmodeus smiled down at me again and said, "I designed this test for you to get what I want, so yes, whatever you choose will happen." He took a breath and said, "Now, choose."

I didn't even have to think about what I would say as I cry-answered him in earnest, "I choose that life over this one, hands down. It's no contest."

The crowd erupted in cheers so loud it was hard to hear myself think.

Really, I hadn't been doing much thinking to begin with as I waited for everything to start over or to blur into existence with all of my painful memories gone from my mind forever.

But that moment never came.

Asmodeus smiled evilly down at me as he said, "Your envious heart is one to be reckoned with. I'm glad I don't plan on fighting you."

Again, I was left speechless, wondering what the fuck was going on as Asmodeus disappeared, and the crowd chanted, "Queen!"

It was so loud I reached up to cover my ears as strong arms lifted me up into the air.

I knew my guys were beneath me, carrying me to the other side of the stadium as if I were crowd surfing or something, but I couldn't for the life of me understand or comprehend how or why everything was happening the way that it was, the way that it had. Why wasn't I reliving the better version of my life when the demon promised me that it could be so?

'Well, he's a fucking demon, Becksy,' my power smarted off at me in my head as I was placed on a stage that hadn't been in the arena before.

Derrick, Adam, Tyler, Absinthe, Brax, the Chief, my dads, and Derrick's dads were all there at the edge of the stage below me, looking up at me proudly as the crowd from the stands descended the stairs and filled in the arena behind them.

The sea of faces I could see was happy and enthusiastic, but I still had tears drying on my cheeks, blood smeared on my clothes, and nasty black shit dripping down my leg from where my dagger was sheathed on my hip.

I just wanted to crawl inside myself, to wallow inside the beauty of what could have been, and mourn the loss of a life I'd evidently, never see. I didn't want to be the center of attention, standing out in the open for everyone to see and gawk at.

But no one asked me what I wanted, not after Asmodeus had, and then never fulfilled his promise.

"Queen Rebecca," someone said from beside me as a hush fell across the ample space.

I turned to look at the man, and instantly, I knew this was no man at all.

'Lucifer,' my power said as I took in his big black wings and utter perfection personified.

"Congratulations. You've passed six out of seven Hell trials, a feat few others have ever accomplished before," Lucifer said as my mouth hung open, yet again.

How the fuck was that possible? I wasn't special; I just did what I thought was right at the time. Is that not what everyone else did when it was their turn to make the decisions?

"Your first trial, you proved that you would murder to protect yourself, and in the second, your wrath could've rivaled even the angriest, most vengeful of my demons.

In your third trial, your pride won it for you before you even made it over to the demon I'd sent to end you, and still, you killed him anyway, a decision I'm still finding myself smiling about.

Your choice to not choose between these men," he said as he gestured to my team, "showed you are greedy enough to keep and love them all despite what anyone else may think of it." Then, conspiratorially, he whispered, "I don't blame you one bit."

Without stopping to pause for longer than an instant, he continued, "In your fifth trial, you killed for selfish reasons, ensuring your survival over that of another who was just as starved and thirsty as you were. You lost the sixth trial because you wouldn't kill an innocent, but you won your seventh by being envious of yourself, no less, and choosing a better life than the one you were born into."

His recap of my wins and loss had my eyes bugging out of my head as I tried to comprehend everything he was saying. Try as I might, though, I had to just accept that I would probably never understand the gauntlet's ways and tried to shift my focus back to what Lucifer was saying.

"We have yet to know if you will pass the gauntlet entirely, but as of right now, we all have high hopes for you," Lucifer continued speaking. "As such, we would like to give you this gift. I know that when the times come, you will need to harness your evil side, and this will help you along the way.

Take it, and may the evil within you never be surmounted by the good inside, only matched."

He gestured to my chest, and I looked down to see a silver chain hanging from my neck with a glass vial filled with purple liquid, resting between my breasts. Absentmindedly, I reached for the item and lifted it to see it better.

I'd never seen metal shaped so elegantly before, but there was no ignoring the absolutely chilling vibe that shivered through me when I looked at the swirling liquid inside the vial.

"There are seven potions that can appear in the vial based on what you need at any given time: destruction, manipulation, influence, lustfulness, resolve, invisibility, and poison. You'll never need to ask it to change, for the potion inside will change on its own; it knows what it needs to do. Trust in it, and it will never fail you."

The crowd had started back up at some point, but I couldn't pay them any mind as I dropped the vial to my chest and glanced up at Lucifer.

"Go now, and please," he said as his eyes took on a pleading gleam, "ensure all this doesn't end for good."

Suddenly, that same pain I'd felt when I'd arrived in Hell to begin with, assaulted me all over again, and I felt myself falling. The pain, the heat, and the cold bombarding my senses anew.

'If this is what it's like to travel between Earth and Hell, count me all the way out,' I thought before blackness took over all of my consciousness.

PART II
INTERMISSION

CHAPTER 8

CHIEF OTTO

When Rebecca was done with her Hell trials, I'd traveled back to Earth with Philippa wrapped tightly in my arms, meeting up with Dragon, Essence, and Raven teams on the beach outside Dragon team's safe house. I was careful not to mention anything stressful in front of Rebecca as I watched Philippa play in the sand; she didn't need any more burdens than the ones she already had to deal with. Still, there was the inescapable fact that their missions still needed to get done. Even though the timing wasn't the greatest, I needed to figure out how I was going to ensure their missions were completed, whether she was going through her gauntlet or not.

As soon as Dragon team had coaxed Rebecca into lying down for a little while, Derrick, Adam, and Tyler all came back outside to talk to us, leaving Brax and Absinthe behind so they could keep an eye on Rebecca.

I wanted to have that talk with Absinthe, but not before I was able to talk to Rebecca face to face, and with the looks of things, I was going to have to wait on all of that until she made it the rest of the way through her gauntlet.

I'd been catching up with the men from the other two teams, but I'd been keeping the conversation light and off any subjects that I knew could stir up the group's mixed emotions.

Raven team, made up of Derrick's dads, were all retired from active service with the hunters, and it'd been a while since I'd seen them last. However, it'd seemed like no time had passed at all when we started talking again, joking in our old familiar way.

On the other hand, Essence team was supposed to be working for Binaria East, and their hostility toward me since they'd been moved over there hadn't gone unnoticed. It may have diminished some over the years, and they were cordial enough as we were standing around talking, but I was undoubtedly picking up hints of the old anger they held since it was apparent they were thinking things they weren't saying.

However, when Derrick, Adam, and Tyler settled into their seats, all conversation turned to Rebecca and her performance in Hell, and any resentment seemed to be forgotten for the time being.

"Is she sleeping?" Logan asked, eyeing the guys where they just sat down.

Adam and Tyler nodded, but it was Derrick who spoke. "Yeah, it took a little bit to get her to relax enough to fall asleep, but she's good now."

Chester looked at his son with a nervous or worried expression as he asked what he wanted to know, not being one to shy away from anything for as long as I'd known him, getting right to the point. "You boys know who you've got in there, right?"

At his question, I wasn't sure whether he was talking about Absinthe or Rebecca; it could've gone either way, really, but as he asked another question before Derrick could answer him, it became clear who he'd meant.

"She's supposed to be the next queen," Chester said as if it were a big secret, which in retrospect, I could see why he'd say it that way.

The Order of Division was ruthless when it came to killing the would-be kings and queens. Though I had no idea why or how they'd missed Rebecca in their unbroken lineage of slaughter, I'd had to start questioning whether the attempts on Rebecca's life had all been orchestrated by Tina, or if The Order had something to do with them as well.

"We suspected she could be when her powers started showing up, but we didn't really have proof until today," Adam answered.

"How's it feel, old man?" Brock asked Brandt as he patted him on the back with a heavy hand, "Being the queen's father?"

Brock from Raven team and Brandt from Essence team were as Viking-looking as one could get in this day and age. I'd thought their familial lines had crossed at some point way back when, and as I watched them side by side, that fact seemed all the more true; the similarities in both their personalities and looks were obvious.

"Well, I don't know yet," Brandt responded with a smile before he patted Brock on the back as well and asked, "How's it feel to be a king's father?"

Laughter erupted from the fathers around the table, but my eyes drifted to the men of Dragon team, and their faces said it all.

They didn't know which of them, if any, Rebecca would choose to be her kings, and I could see the worry that uncertainty caused them hanging over them like a dark cloud.

"We don't know we're going to be her kings yet," Tyler said with a bit of an attitude. "So, just keep your assumptions to yourself for now, huh?"

I could see his remark cause a few head turns, but no one said anything. However, I knew Tyler, and since his parents died, he'd always met new situations and self-doubt with anger. It was just a part of who he was now, as if he was never open-minded or optimistic about anything at first glance and always had to take the time to come around.

I knew it had been hard for him to come around to the rest of his team over the time they'd been working together, but even from my distanced position, I could see that Rebecca was changing even that deep-seated damage living within him.

I glanced over to check on Philippa, where she was still fascinated with the sand on the beach before I cleared my throat to get everyone's attention. "That is a problem for another day, I'm afraid," I started, pulling everyone's gaze to me. "We have more pressing concerns that need to be addressed."

They were all quiet as they waited for me to elaborate, but I didn't miss it when each of the boys of Dragon team tensed up, almost as if they thought I was going to task them with something. However, I felt their tension leave them as I turned my attention to the other teams' men.

"I'm assuming you all know that we're dealing with different circumstances here than those that usually occur for an initiate." I waited for them to nod in my direction before I continued. "Rebecca is already bound to her teammates, and you know the pull the gauntlet has on the family members of an initiate going through it. There's no way I can ask them to complete their missions while Rebecca is still in the gauntlet or even during her intermission. It would be heartless of me to ask that of them."

I could see the wheels turning in the minds of all the men in front of me, but I could also see that they understood where I was going with this, and no one seemed to mind. As I spelled out what I needed from each of them, firm head nods answered me with unspoken resolve as if we'd stepped back in time to a place where they were used to taking orders from me, and I felt it in my soul that this was the right course of action to take.

"I know none of you still work for me, and you don't owe me your loyalty, but I'm asking for it anyway because your children need this of you. Dragon team's missions are of the utmost importance, and there's a timeline involved here that even a gauntlet can't slow down. If you guys were to handle these missions while Rebecca is otherwise occupied, it would continue the efforts they've already put in to hold off the apocalypse."

Each of the men looked to their teammates, including the guys of

Dragon team, though their faces looked more relieved than anything else.

"We've been dying to get back in the saddle," Liam of Raven team said. "Just point us where you need us, Chief."

I nodded at them, accepting the gift they were giving so willingly, and turned to look at Essence team to see if they too would offer up their help.

Logan, Ben, and Brandt all stepped to the side so we couldn't hear their conversation for a moment, but when they came back, Ben announced, "On one condition, we come back to Binaria West."

"Done," I said, knowing full well that I would gladly take them back now that Tina wasn't there to endanger them anymore. It had been the reason I'd sent them to the other side of the world in the first place - so that whoever the traitor was wouldn't be able to harm them like they had Rebecca's real parents. I also knew that the monumental undertaking of restructuring both Binaria West and Binaria East would require as many loyal hunters as we could possibly get on our side. I'd actually already planned on pulling them back over here anyway.

"Then what are the missions, Chief?" Ben asked with a smile that told me he was happy to be back on this side of the planet; way more, in fact, than he was actually letting on.

I took a deep breath as I considered his question but ended up just lifting my hand in Dragon team's direction as I said, "Guys, I think you would be better able to explain everything that you have going on than I would. Derrick, why don't you delegate everything out to them?"

Derrick's face was stunned, and the looks on his father's faces were proud as I said that. I knew why. I'd been grooming Derrick to take my place since he was born, frequently imagining that he would do a much better job than me if he could only learn to see the gray area in things rather than just the black and white facts of any situation presented to him. I didn't give him the reins lightly, and I wouldn't have at all if I hadn't seen changes in him recently.

He wasn't so quick to judge anymore, or he was at least thinking things through longer than he usually did, which was a win in my book. But it was his way with Tyler that had really sealed the deal for me on deciding that now was the right time to hand over some of my power to him.

He and Tyler had never gotten along well, and I was never sure it was entirely Tyler's or Derrick's fault; it had been a mixture of both.

The gauntlet is traumatic for everyone.

When Tyler went through his, winning five out of seven in both Heaven and Hell, just like Derrick and Adam had, I'd seen how proud his parents were of him, how happy he was to be put on a team that was steadily building up to be the best one in my ranks.

However, Tyler lost his parents right after his gauntlet, right when he was still reeling from what he'd been through, right when he moved from his parents' house and into the safe house Derrick and Adam were staying in.

Derrick had just been given the responsibility of leading a team of broken but brilliant individuals and was only trying to be successful, trying to live up to the expectations we'd all been putting on him.

I thought that's really what caused all of their animosity toward each other, the fact that they'd never really started off on the right foot.

However, after they told me about everything that had happened while they were fighting Tina and all that followed in the wake of that battle, I realized there was finally something linking Derrick and Tyler together in a way they'd never been connected before.

I couldn't help the smile on my face as Derrick stood and handed out orders like a pro, while Adam disclosed what he'd seen in his visions, and Tyler added in the best way to go about the missions logistically.

They were finally acting like the team I'd always envisioned them becoming. I found myself staring at them just as proudly as all the other fathers were, and I saw Rebecca's and Brax's faces in my mind as the responsible parties for eliciting the change within their teammates.

For a moment there, I really thought we had a chance at changing everything, and as I watched the other teams disappear from the beach, missions on their minds, I couldn't help but have hope for the future because it seemed like we might actually be getting one.

CHAPTER 9

BECKS

My mind was hazy, but my body felt amazing, wrapped in warm blankets on a soft bed as I snuggled tighter into the sheets, wiggling my toes some and reveling in the comfort I felt. There was no pain, my body was the perfect temperature, and nothing in the world was wrong at all for a few beautiful, blissful seconds.

Slowly, voices began to register in my brain, but as what they were saying became more apparent, I closed my eyes shut and wished as hard as I could for sleep to retake me.

"It's only a twenty-four-hour intermission, Absinthe!" Brax's gravelly voice said in quieted anger as if he were trying to keep his voice down. "And she's already been asleep for almost four of those hours!"

"She needs her rest, Brax," Absinthe said, but then paused before he chuckled. "Oh well, she's awake now anyway."

My eyes shot open, wondering how in the world he knew that, but as five different weights landed on my bed, I knew I couldn't avoid the inevitable any longer, no matter how much I wanted to.

"Hey, Sleepyhead," Brax said as I sat up in the center of the bed and took in everyone around me.

Brax was on my left, sitting way too close to me, but such was his way. Derrick was sitting on my right, staring down at me with a small smile playing on his lips. Adam sat down next to Brax while Tyler sat on the other side of Derrick. To my surprise, Absinthe climbed on my bed as well and sat cross-legged at the foot of it with a knowing smile.

All of the guys' eyes being on me at once was still difficult to think around. Yet, over time, I'd seen I was already getting used to it, getting better at handling the overwhelming emotions that flooded me every time it happened.

"Four hours is nowhere near enough sleep after what I just went through," I said to no one in particular, and a few sarcastic chuckles sounded from the men surrounding me in response.

"I know," Derrick said sympathetically. "You could probably sleep the entire twenty-four hours in between the trials, and it still wouldn't be enough."

I nodded at him because I fully believed everything he said was true. I knew I felt awesome, better than I had in a while, but I also knew if I was given a chance, I would've slept for a hell of a lot longer.

"We were talking about it before," Brax said, "but we've come to the decision that what you do with your intermission should be your choice. If you want to sleep the whole time, we'll make sure no one disturbs you. If you want to train, we can do that too. None of us are going to pressure you either way, though. What you just went through…" He didn't finish his thought as his eyes rolled up to the ceiling as if he couldn't find the right words.

"You did great, but you were put through a lot," Adam finished for him, and I could tell by the relieved look on Brax's face that he was appreciative of Adam's interjection.

I glanced around at each of them, and though I knew I could sleep, I didn't want to.

I hadn't been able to tell them goodbye before I was thrown into Hell without warning, and I didn't want to risk that happening again when I was inevitably sent to Heaven the same way. However, I didn't think I had the energy, or at least, I didn't want to spend the energy I did have on training the whole time either.

"Are those my only choices? Sleeping or training?" I asked everyone at once.

Tyler chuckled some before he asked, "What'd you have in mind, Hot Stuff?"

I smiled as a plan developed in my mind, and as everyone saw the wheels turning in my head through my connection with Brax and their connection with him, each of their faces matched my own.

MEMORIES FROM HELL'S part of the gauntlet kept trying to spring to the forefront of my mind, especially the images of the life I should've had that Asmodeus showed me. It was like my brain was screaming for me to make sense of it all, to take a minute to just go through everything that'd happened, but I didn't have time for the 'breakdown' that I knew would inevitably follow.

You don't spend most of your life in an asylum without learning the pitfalls of your own psychology, the aspects of life that can rip the floor out from beneath you.

"Spending too much time thinking and fantasizing about how life should be, or what could have been, sends you to your dark place, Rebecca," one of the doctors had told me while I was there. "You need to keep yourself from going there by finding something else to focus on."

She wasn't necessarily wrong.

I could literally spend hours sitting in a corner, imagining a life full of all the things I thought would make me happy, stuck in memories of running with fairies or hiding from werewolves. The whole time, I knew I had this dumbass smile on my face while the images floated through my consciousness. I'd even gotten so lost in it at times that I'd forgotten to eat or that life was apparently still going on around me.

However, as soon as the curtain would drop, and I was somehow pulled out of my own head, reality would sink in, leaving a bitter, sad, and lonely taste in my mouth. I would look around at the asylum after having spent all day in my imagination, and my heart would sink, my soul shattering inside my chest as I realized those fantasies weren't real.

As the doctors liked to call it, my 'dark place' always showed up as the perfect hideaway for my mind to retreat to after stressful situations or prolonged periods of being stuck in my own head. However, though that doctor may have been right about how those situations sent me there and why, her opinion that it was altogether negative, through and through, was completely wrong in my opinion.

Yes, my dark place was where I'd been when death seemed like the best option compared to the reality I was in, but it was also a beautiful place where I wasn't crazy, and no one was telling me otherwise. It was where I knew what was real and what wasn't, where reality met and greeted my imagination in understanding and acceptance, where the two coincided in harmony.

Granted, that harmony had made me want to off myself as the only reasonable alternative to living in sadness, but it was beautiful darkness nonetheless. I would never deny that.

However, I still had the intermission and all of Heaven's trials to get through. If I stopped and thought too hard and long about the monster I became with my adoptive parents, the apparitions I killed, or the images Asmodeus showed me, I knew I'd go back to that dark place and stay there for entirely too long.

I couldn't go there; not when I had a team I cared about relying on me, or well, an entire world as it were. So, I did what I had to do to keep my emotional state in check; I compartmentalized. I threw all of what happened to the back of my mind to deal with later.

Right now, all I really wanted to do was spend some alone time with each of the men in my life and my familiar, and dammit, they'd finally asked me what I wanted for once; there was no way I was going to let that opportunity slip through my fingers.

I told them I wanted to spend time with each of them, and though their eyes lit up at my words, they also reminded me that I was on a timetable, that if we were going to do things this way, we needed to plan it out so that everyone got the same amount of time with me. Of course, it needed to be fair for everyone, but the fact that they cared enough and desired time with me for themselves in the first place had my belly flipping again.

Tyler said something cocky then about the order in which I chose to see them having some kind of hierarchy to it, but I shut that shit down quick.

"All of you need to go to separate places, and when I'm ready to spend my time with you, I'll show up. There's no order of importance with me; you all need to know that," I said, and it'd had the effect I'd wanted.

Tyler went to his room, Adam strolled to the kitchen, and Derrick went out onto the beach with Absinthe trailing behind him. Brax glanced at me with a sad look on his face, probably because he was going to have to share the time I had left with them, but moved outside swiftly, never mentioning his own thoughts because he knew what I needed right then.

Instead of focusing on that nagging part of my brain that was still trying to escape the mental box I'd stuffed it in, I tried to figure out who I would go see first, hoping no one would take my choice as a slight against them in some way.

I was still wearing what I'd made appear in the gauntlet - my black t-shirt and shorts, but there was no more blood, sweat, or anything on them as if it had all been an apparition too, and I huffed as I looked down at myself.

Each of the guys brought unique things to the table with their completely distinct personalities speaking to me differently. They were all mysteries in some form or another, but I already knew how each of them affected me, and I had to consider how delicate my emotional state was before I chose who to see first.

Not considering Absinthe's abrupt entrance into the whole dynamic, the rest of us had shared a beautiful night together in the incubus lair not too long ago. However, just as I didn't have time to process Hell's part of the gauntlet now, I hadn't had time to process fully after that night, either. We'd just gotten overwhelmed by the lives we'd been living and saving the world and whatnot.

All of our proclamations to each other had happened before we actually got physically intimate, and we hadn't really discussed it afterward either. What if, once they'd had me, they'd changed their minds? What if I wasn't any good, and they knew they could find better elsewhere? Like maybe with a hunter that had more experience than me, both in real life and in the bedroom.

'Ugh, stop worrying so damn much,' I told myself and set about what I needed to be figuring out right then.

I knew Derrick would probably offer the task list I needed to focus my attention, running me through all the bullet points in his head about what I'd be facing next, all while he hid his real emotions behind that stern facade he always wore.

I'd seen past it a few times, and it pleased me to no end when I made cracks in his mask, but I wasn't ready to face what else I needed to do right then.

Absinthe was his own Pandora's box of unanswered questions, and my complicated emotions when it came to him weren't things I thought I'd be able to handle. At least, not yet. Yes, I needed more answers from him, and I needed to figure out how my power thought I loved him already, but I was in no headspace to try and sort that through.

I already knew I wanted to save my time with Brax for last, and through our connection, I was sure he knew it too.

'Ugh, why does every choice have to come with an entire mental flow chart of possible consequences?' I thought with a sigh as I wished for my life to be easier before I quickly decided who I needed right then.

I COULD HEAR his music as I stepped into the hallway, and like a moth to a flame, I was drawn to the rhythmic and melodic sounds of Tyler's guitar.

My belly was doing something weird, and my palms were sweating as I stood outside his door, trying to build up the courage I needed just to walk in. I took a deep breath with my eyes shut before I reached for the doorknob. When I stepped into his room, I had a moment of hesitation, a moment where I started second-guessing whether he really wanted me there.

However, when his green eyes rose to meet mine, his fingers faltered for a second on the chords he was playing, I was spurred closer to him, a shiver going through me that had me closing the door and moving to sit on the end of his bed.

He kept playing as he stared at me, a questioning look on his face as if he was asking whether I wanted him to stop or not. "Keep playing," I said as my eyes drifted to his deft fingers, where they were moving over the strings with well-practiced ease.

Tyler nodded, his hat nearly pointing to the floor as his eyes drifted slowly down my body before they settled on some spot on the floor next to the bed.

I couldn't name the song he was playing, and I got the strange impression that he'd come up with it on his own, but I had no idea how I knew that.

Everything about it screamed Tyler though, the deep and true tones made up of an equal balance of uplifting sadness, and something about it spoke directly to my soul. Like he was playing the sounds that should've accompanied my thoughts and feelings.

I closed my eyes so his image wouldn't distract me from thoroughly enjoying the sounds he was making, and tilted my head back as I listened. However, no sooner had I done that than he was stopping, causing me to look back at him questioningly.

His eyes were locked on mine, and I didn't know what to do with myself under the weight of his gaze. I felt my face get hot, and my palms started sweating all over again.

"What?" I asked with, no doubt, a full-on blush tinting my cheeks.

My question seemed to snap Tyler out of wherever his brain had gone in that moment, and he said, "One sec," before he was reaching over to the nightstand to grab his phone.

He pressed on it a few times before he raised his other hand to his lips, making a shhh sound toward me before he pressed something else on his phone. After quickly setting it down on the bed between us, he started playing again, and I knew he was recording himself.

I didn't know why he chose that moment to start recording his song, but I didn't make a sound because I didn't want to mess him up. He probably needed it for something if I had to guess. I'd watched a documentary one time about how musicians regularly record themselves so they can play different melodies and then merge them all together to make a well-rounded song, even though only one person was playing.

If that was what he was doing, I was there for it. The boy had a way with that guitar that I just couldn't get enough of, and before long, I was tilting my head back again as I listened intently.

It was over too quickly. After only a few minutes or so, I watched as Tyler picked up his phone again. With his other hand, he grabbed his guitar and sat it down next to the bed, propping it up against the nightstand while I tried to ignore the pang in my heart I felt when I realized he was apparently done playing.

A few seconds later, the song he'd just recorded started playing through the speaker on his phone, and all I could do was look at him as he left it playing and set it on the nightstand, sliding back on the bed, so his back was resting against the wall.

He threw both of his legs up onto the bed in the space between us, spreading them some, and then wiggled his finger at me in a come here motion.

I knew what he meant, but in my head, for some reason, I didn't believe he actually wanted me to move closer to him, so my body didn't move; I just kind of stared at him.

I didn't know what had me hesitating, and I certainly didn't know why I was all of a sudden overwhelmed by his presence like he was taking up way more space in the room than his body actually filled, but I was, all the same.

Surprising me with the level of demand I heard in his voice, he said, "Come here," and as if I were hypnotized, I was crawling up the bed toward him. My eyes couldn't figure out how to leave his, but when I was right between his legs on my hands and knees, looking him right in the face, he handled that problem for me.

He sent each of his hands out and twirled me around, forcing me to sit with my back to his chest. As soon as the shock of the swift motion began to wear off, a smile I couldn't prevent spread across my lips, and I looked down so my hair would fall and hide my face.

"Uh uh," Tyler said as his right hand slid my hair behind my ear and then pulled my chin up and around so I would look at him. "You know you do that too much, right?"

"What?"

"Look down. Like I don't deserve to see the smile I caused on your face."

My mind short-circuited completely in that moment.

"It's rude, really," he said with just a hint of a smile playing on his lips as his finger started tracing my jawline.

A small, involuntary, and shaky gasp pulled air into my lungs as I stared at Tyler and watched as his entire demeanor began to change.

His face became serious, almost angry, as he looked at me and said, "You may hide everything you feel with everyone else, but not here. Not with me."

I think my breathing stopped altogether at that, but he wasn't done, and I found myself hanging on every word he said as if my life depended on it.

"When you're with me, you're mine," he said as he cupped my chin, not too hard, but definitely hard enough to capture all of my attention. "And I want to see everything I do to you. I want to know how I make you feel. From how you smile when you think I won't notice, to how you're blushing right now. I want all of it."

The song he'd recorded was playing on repeat, and as it started over again, Tyler licked his lips and looked at mine, the heat in my stomach only getting hotter, the tingles on my skin only spreading further with every second that passed.

His lips touched mine then in a slow and passionate kiss that I returned with ease. It had just a hint of tongue, and I knew at that moment I'd never get enough of it, of kissing Tyler. Something about the way he was holding me, the words he'd said, and the way he was kissing me as if we had all the time in the world, nearly had my heart exploding in my chest.

His hands started sliding down my sides lightly, drawing small circles beneath the hem of my shirt. Something inside me made me act bolder than I felt, and I turned around, making sure to keep our kiss going as I straddled his lap and sent my hands up to either side of his face.

Tyler moaned a little into my mouth, and it was that sound mixed with his music and the racing of my heart that became my undoing. I was lost to him thoroughly, entirely at his mercy, and I couldn't find it in me to care about the level of control he had over me right then. I craved the attention he was giving me, the passion I felt pouring out of him, so when he pulled me even closer to him, I let him lead me where he wanted me to go because I wanted it too.

I wanted Tyler with everything I had.

CHAPTER 10

BECKS

"We've got to stop, Babe," Tyler said a little while later as he pulled himself back, eyes closed like he couldn't look at me while he said it.

He'd flipped me over onto my back, and our makeout session had taken on a blinding intensity that I never wanted to end, but as he pulled away, something about the expression on his face had me pausing, wondering what I'd done wrong.

When he looked back down at me, he said, "You can't have sex during your intermission. It takes too much out of you."

"Well, that's bullshit," I said without thinking, my anger at the entire concept of the gauntlet not getting any better as time went on.

My words had a laugh flowing out of Tyler's mouth as he sat back down on the bed and rubbed a hand down his face, letting that piece of hair fall back in his eyes again.

I couldn't bring myself to get up yet, a decision made completely based on angry spite at the situation. Instead, I crossed my arms over my chest and stared up at the ceiling.

"Hey," Tyler said, getting my attention back. "You know I want to, though, right?"

Immediately, I blushed again but still had enough wits about me to nod back at him in response. "Well, you're going to need to distract me with something else then. All this," I said as I gestured to myself, "isn't just gonna calm down on its own."

Tyler laughed again and said, "Mine's not either." He seemed contemplative for a moment before he suggested, "How about I teach you a few chords?"

At that moment, I was sure my eyes lit up like a Christmas tree. I'd never played an instrument before, never even been allowed to get close to one other than Tyler's guitar. But had I ever gotten a choice to learn to play something, it definitely would've been the guitar. It just spoke so many different emotions, almost like it spoke a million other languages solely based on who was playing what at any given time.

Tyler's smile was instant as he saw my reaction, and as he handed me the instrument and cut off the song playing on his phone, I knew I was going to enjoy this. Maybe not as much as I would've enjoyed sex with Tyler, but it was definitely going to come in as a close second.

A LITTLE BIT LATER, my fingertips were sore, and my brain felt a bit overloaded, but I'd learned a great deal and was already playing something that resembled music to the untrained ear. I was pretty proud of myself, but after a while, the fact that all the other guys were waiting for me to show up became so nagging on my mind that I had to say goodbye to Tyler so everyone else didn't feel slighted. I didn't want to leave him, but I was still excited to hang out with everyone else; it was a very weird feeling I'd never really experienced before.

Surprising me again, because that was just what Tyler did, he pulled me in for a slow kiss before I walked out of his room. I knew he meant it to be a sweet and thoughtful gesture, but it only made leaving him harder in reality.

Still, I left his room anyway and headed to the kitchen where

Adam was sitting at the bar, staring at his phone with the most bored-looking face I'd ever seen him wear. It was actually pretty funny, and as I rounded the corner from the hallway, a small giggle escaped me as I watched him.

His eyes shot up to mine instantly, and a warm smile spread on those big lips of his.

"Are you coming to spend time with me, or just passing through to get to someone else?"

His tone and the words he said had no jealousy or anger within them. I knew he was just genuinely wondering what my plans were, but still, a pang of hurt seeped through me at the question.

However, I tried to ignore it as I took the stool next to him and said, "Nope, I'm with you for right now." My smile was light, and the questioning look on Adam's face told me he knew something had affected me, but we both moved past it quickly.

"Are you hungry?" he asked, and as soon as the words left his mouth, food was almost all I could think about as flashbacks from the hunger I felt in the gauntlet broke out of my mental box like a fucking jack-in-the-box.

"I'll take that as a yes," he said with a small chuckle as he climbed down from his stool, apparently seeing my answer written on my face without me ever needing to say a word.

He made his way over to the fridge, and after a few seconds, he started pulling out all kinds of ingredients, laying each one out on the counter in front of me. When he was done, he stood with his hands planted on the edge of the counter and looked me right in the eyes as he said, "Alright, get over here."

"What?" the word fell out of my mouth before I could stop it.

Adam's bright smile lit up his face again as he said, "You need to learn how to cook, and I'm going to teach you, so get over here." There was no timidity in his command, no hesitation, and nothing to suggest he doubted I'd go along with his instructions, and as I found myself climbing down from my stool, a small shiver went all the way through me.

"I might burn this place down. You know that, right?" I asked as I stood beside him and looked down at the ingredients before me, wondering what in the world he was having me make.

"No, you won't," Adam said as he handed me a knife and set me up with a head of lettuce by the cutting board. "Not with vegetables at least," he laughed again as he showed me how to cut up the lettuce for a salad.

It wasn't too tricky, but I was still scared I was going to chop one of my fingers off. However, after a little bit, I felt like I'd finally gotten the hang of it and moved on to the other vegetables without much more instruction.

Adam grabbed two beers out of the fridge and opened them, setting one in front of me while he sipped from the other. He hopped up onto the empty part of the counter to watch my movements and said, "You did really good in Hell. I'm proud of you."

His words and the sincerity I heard in them made me glance up at him for a second. He was staring down at me with a soft, sad-ish smile, and for the life of me, I couldn't figure out why my doing well in Hell's trials would make him sad.

"Thanks, but what's that face for?" I asked, and then immediately looked back down to what I was doing so he wouldn't feel my eyes on him as he answered.

It took him a second, I guessed, so he could decide if he wanted to tell me what he was thinking, but finally came around. "I want to tell you what I've seen in my visions, but I know I can't. At least not where you're concerned. Nothing is clear or for sure at this point, and it's just a little unnerving is all."

I thought about that for a second before I replied. "Your visions are only going to come true if they're super clear to you, right?"

"Right."

"How often are your visions really clear?"

He paused for a second to take another swig from his beer before he answered. "It's hit or miss depending on how many moving parts there are." I must have looked confused because he hurried to explain further as if he didn't mean for that to sound vague. "For example, when there are a whole lot of decisions that a bunch of people need to make, my visions are always pretty cloudy because any one of those decisions could change everything. But if there are only a few variables, or if the decisions have already been decided, they get really clear."

"I guess that makes sense."

Our conversation stopped for a little bit then so he could lead me through mixing up the salad ingredients, cubing the chicken thighs, and setting the pasta water to a boil, but we flowed right back into where we left off once everything was going again.

"Have you always been able to see the future?" I asked.

Adam chuckled somewhat darkly before he answered. "Yeah, but my visions were hardly ever reliable enough before I got the rest of my powers after the gauntlet."

Not wanting to ignore those small tells of his, I asked, "What was that laugh about?"

He seemed surprised that I'd caught it or that I'd questioned him on it but sighed and answered anyway.

"I've had a crazy life so far, Becks, and sometimes my visions have helped me, but there have been times where they've caused nothing but pain," he said, and I could hear the sincerity in his voice. However, I kept my eyes off him because he seemed to be more comfortable talking that way.

"Would you mind telling me about it?" I asked softly, trying not to let my face show how much I wanted to know everything about him, even the upsetting parts.

"You want my life story in twenty minutes?" he asked with a chuckle, and I nodded without looking up.

He didn't say anything for a minute, though. Instead, he hopped down from the counter and told me he'd take over from there.

I was disappointed that he didn't feel like he could tell me about his past, but as I was washing the chicken from my hands in the sink, I felt a bit better when he said, "Sorry, I'll teach you how to cook later, I promise. I just need to be doing something with my hands if we're diving into all this. It'll keep me focused on the here and now."

I smiled and said, "I can understand that completely," as I turned around to face him after drying my hands.

He reached out and picked me up, setting me down on the counter where he'd been sitting before. I didn't complain, and I didn't say anything as he started talking.

"I was the middle kid," he said with a smile. "I've got two older brothers and two younger sisters, but I never felt that middle-child-syndrome you always hear people talk about. I wasn't forgotten or ignored as others from large families have been."

He put the pasta in the water before he continued. "Just like this team does, my family means the world to me; you all ground me, I guess, is the best way to say it."

I nodded, but he wasn't looking.

"When it comes to you guys or my siblings, there's nothing I wouldn't do for any of them, and they all know it. It's why my youngest sister is always asking me to intervene on her behalf to our parents when she's done something or wants something."

I was smiling, trying to process that Adam came from a large family, and kicking myself for not reading through their files still. *'Like, come on, Becks. You know you should've read them by now,'* I thought but didn't say anything while Adam kept talking.

"'You're the golden boy,' she'll say. 'I know if you tell Mom and Dad that the party will be fine, they'll let me go. Please ask them for me, Adam,'" he'd kicked his voice up an octave to mimic his sister, and it made me giggle at him.

"I really am a pushover when it comes to Alicia, and I couldn't care less about the consequences," he chuckled right along with me. "My other sister, Marcia, is a different beast, though. She has a troubled past like me, and because of it, we've always been closer than any of our other siblings are. No one else could or would even try to see or stomp out Marcia's darkness like I would.

It got worse when we were teenagers, and my parents, at their wit's end, would say things like, 'I just don't understand her! Adam, can you go make her get dressed already?'

I'd go upstairs and just stand outside her door. We didn't have ESP or anything, but somehow, she just knew it was me, and she'd let me in."

I had no idea how what he was telling me applied to the visions I'd asked about, but I didn't want to stop him and ask, so I didn't.

"Sometimes, words were necessary, like I'd need to ask her if she woke up crying again." He was utterly lost to the story as he kept cooking, and I was no better as I watched him and listened.

"I've asked her that more times than I could count. She'd be standing there all red-eyed and puffy-faced, hair disheveled, nodding at me before she'd break down crying.

Other times, it was quiet that she needed; just her big brother, the one who'd found her that night, the only one who'd seen her in her most vulnerable and terrified state."

He got quiet then, and for a moment, I didn't think he was going to tell me any more, so I pried gently. "What happened to her?"

His hands stilled over the pot he was stirring, but he answered anyway.

"She'd been taken, and I was the one who found her. Blood had dried where her captors had cauterized what was left of her fingers just so they could do the same on her other hand. You can still see the scars from the shackles she'd been chained with on her wrists and ankles if you know where to look."

He shook his head as if he were trying to shake away the memories before he glanced up at me and said, "She's one of the strongest people I know to have made it through all that."

I nodded, not wanting to break the spell that had him talking, and as he kept moving around the kitchen, his words started to make more sense.

"It was partly my fault that she was there for so long because as hard as I tried to force a vision to find her, as hard as my parents pushed me for any possible information about who'd taken her or why, for nearly a year, nothing would come to me.

I couldn't understand why my visions had abandoned me when I needed them most. But now, any time I get all sad or start feeling bad about myself, Marcia won't have it. She'll say things like, 'If I can't go to a dark place, neither can you.' And every time, it stops when she says that. Like what right do I have, dwelling on finding her that way when she was the one who'd had to live it?"

My mouth was hanging open, and I couldn't *not* speak my mind right then.

"Just because your trauma isn't the same as someone else's, doesn't mean that what you went through wasn't traumatic in its own right."

He looked up at me and something passed between us. Some emotion I wasn't smart enough to name.

"Thank you, Becks," he said after the moment had passed, but I could tell he was struggling to believe what I'd said.

After a few beats of silence, he picked up where he'd left off before I interrupted him.

"My older brothers, Aaron and Malachi, were always off doing their own things or tormenting me while we were growing up. I don't talk to them much anymore, but for holidays and special occasions, but I know that they're only a phone call away if I need them, and they know the reverse is true of me as well.

I blame most of our lack of closeness on that year Marcia was missing, though.

I was under constant pressure from my parents, their team members, and even the hunters' higher-ups to figure out what had happened to Marcia. Being young and temperamental, my brothers got it in their heads one day that I was deliberately holding back information from everyone. Though that was true to a certain extent, if I'd seen anything that could have remotely led to her whereabouts, I would have said something.

I didn't tell people what I did see because I didn't want anyone to know that Marcia was being tortured for information by demons. I'd thought I was protecting my parents by only telling them that she was alive and in danger.

But Aaron and Malachi didn't believe me, and they put me through their own form of torture to make me talk, but I knew if I did, it would wreck everything and everyone in our family until she was found. So, despite their attempts, I kept what I knew to myself."

I didn't know what to say to Adam in that moment. I could hardly wrap my mind around what he'd said, much less figure out how to help him in any way.

"Later, when Marcia did finally come home, and everyone found out what had happened to her, my brothers looked at me differently. It was as if they finally realized what I'd been hiding, yet also couldn't find it in themselves to apologize to me for what they'd put me through.

I mean, I know they finally respected me, but we were never the same after that. Never close. They were too 'stubborn and prideful' as Marcia would put it."

As he handed me a plate of chicken pasta, I looked down as if it had appeared out of nowhere because I'd been so lost in what Adam was saying, I hadn't even noticed he was finished and had already straightened up.

"Why don't we go sit down?" he asked, and I followed him over to the table and sat down next to him.

"How old were you when she went missing?" I asked.

Adam finished chewing the bite of food he'd already put in his mouth before he answered. "I was eight."

My heart felt like a weight was pulling it down to the ground as I imagined a little eight-year-old Adam in that situation, seeing all those terrible things happening to his sister and having that much pressure on him.

"They told me I basically have 'survivor's guilt' or whatever," he said after a minute, but a lump had formed in my throat, so I couldn't speak right then.

"Apparently, my time undercover in the army just added to it."

"Wait, you were in the army, too?" I finally got my voice to work.

He smiled down at his plate and said, "Yeah. It's not all it's cracked up to be."

Despite myself, I giggled at the way he'd said that, and he smiled right back at me over his food.

Taking a bite for myself, I asked, "Do you want to tell me about that too?"

He looked a little put out like he was exasperated, and I rushed to say, "You don't have to if you don't want to. I'm sorry. Gah, just ignore me," and looked back down to my plate so he wouldn't see how I felt on my face.

He'd literally just told me some of the saddest shit I'd ever heard in my life, and there I was, asking him to tell me even more. I would've blamed it on something other than me if I'd had the chance, but I knew it was just the simple fact that I wanted to learn as much as I could about these guys, spurring me on.

"Hey," he said as he reached out a hand to lay it over mine where it laid on the table between us. "I'll tell you everything you want to know, no questions asked. I just feel like my past is nothing but a sore subject, and I don't want to spoil the time we have by bringing up painful ghosts from the past."

At that, I knew exactly what to say because in that moment, I knew Adam better than I ever had before, and the things we'd had in common couldn't be ignored. "My past is nothing but pain too. I hear you guys talk about your families or the experiences you've had, and all I can do is sit there and listen because I don't have anything to add that won't bring the whole mood down. If anyone can understand painful shit, I'd think it would be me.

If you want to talk about it, I want to hear about it, but don't *not* tell me because you think it'll make me sad or ruin our time together or something. If anything, I feel closer to you now than I have before," I said, knowing I was blushing from admitting how I felt, but even more than I wanted to safeguard my own feelings right then, I needed Adam to realize he could tell me anything.

Adam's whole body visibly relaxed as he sighed, staring at me as if he was seeing me for the first time. "You don't know what that means to me."

His hand came up to rub his thumb over my cheekbone, and I found myself leaning toward him without thinking about it.

As he closed the distance between us, his lips fell on mine in one of the most passionate kisses I'd ever felt before. It felt like there was a literal weight attached to it, a weight I wanted so much, I never wanted to live without it, as if it were actually strengthening the bond we shared as our lips danced with one another.

We separated about a minute later and just stared at each other, but for some reason, the act didn't seem weird or uncomfortable at all; it just felt right, and I didn't want it to end.

However, the magic of that moment started receding a short time later, and when Adam turned his head, looking down at the empty plates in front of us, a longing to feel that feeling again settled deep within me.

"How about we clean all this up, and then we can go lay down and talk about whatever you want? How does that sound?"

I agreed quickly and helped with the cleanup, so it took hardly any time at all, but when we were finally walking into his room, I had another moment of hesitation, kind of like how I'd felt when I went into Tyler's room.

However, this time, it wasn't about whether Adam wanted me there or not like it had been with Tyler; it was nervousness about the possibilities that could happen that I felt.

Possibilities and questions ran through my head at an alarming speed as we walked the short distance to his bed. Things like, 'Is he okay with me being in his bed with him? Would he tell me if it wasn't okay? Does he want to hold me? Do I want to be held in the first place? Maybe it would be better if I just sat in the chair at his desk instead, then I wouldn't be putting either of us in an uncomfortable situation. But what if he does want me to be near him?'

My thoughts shut their unrelenting mouth up when he grabbed my hand. Adam pulled me with him to his bed, climbed onto it, and laid down, basically deciding how I laid next to him with how he directed me where he wanted me.

With my head on his chest, one of his arms wrapped around behind me, his other hand draped over my forearm where it laid on his chest too, a contented sigh escaped me as I relaxed into him.

It was crazy how he had that calming effect on me - how one second, I was literally going out of my mind with worry, and within the next, he was silencing all of that without me ever having to say anything in the first place.

There was a subtle beauty in that security, that safe haven he was offering me, and I was entirely too selfish not to take him up on it.

"Can I ask you a question this time?" Adam asked softly, his velvety voice sliding over me.

I couldn't have denied him then if I'd wanted to. "Yeah, what do you want to know?" I asked, surprised with how willing I was to open up to him.

He sighed deeply, making my head rise and fall with the lift in his chest from the movement. "That night in the incubus lair," he started, and immediately my pulse began to quicken just thinking about that night. "Did you...," there was a small pause before he asked, "did you enjoy it?"

I started laughing at the absurdity of that question, but as I looked up at Adam to tell him just how amazing it had been, I suddenly realized that he was taking my laughter as some sort of sick joke, and it knocked my giggles off instantly.

Looking him in the eyes and making sure I had his full attention, I said, "I wasn't laughing because I thought it was bad. I was laughing because just the fact that you would even question such a thing when I enjoyed it so much was almost sarcastically funny."

His eyes seemed to soften somewhat, but he didn't look altogether convinced, so I continued and tried to speak plainly. "I would say that I've had exactly two 'best days' of my life. The first was when I met Brax, and the second was that night. I loved almost every minute I spent with you guys, and yes, I thoroughly enjoyed myself."

His smile told me he believed me. He sighed while he pushed my head back down onto his chest playfully, and I found myself giggling again.

"Okay," he said, verbally accepting what I'd said before he asked, "So what else do you want to know?"

"Can 'everything' be an answer?"

We both laughed some at that, but as soon as we both sobered somewhat, I asked, "Can you tell me the rest of your life story? I know it's been longer than twenty minutes, but I'd really like to know."

He didn't seem put out by the question, probably because he was already expecting it, and when he answered, I found myself listening intently yet again.

"I went through the gauntlet when I was sixteen, and I'd apparently done so well that the chief himself assigned me to go undercover and see what demons were wreaking havoc in Iraq and Afghanistan. I'd known that solo missions were rare and highly respected deals for the hunters, so I'd gone willingly, with an overinflated ego, if I do say so myself." He chuckled some at his own self-deprecating joke.

"I hadn't really gotten good at recognizing the difference between the visions I'd have since my new powers had just kicked in."

I nodded, and the movement on his chest made him pause for a second. He started rubbing his hand on my back in smooth circles as he talked, and I listened.

"So, I joined the Army pretending to be some small-town kid from Oklahoma. I'd always looked older than I actually was, so it only took a few forged documents and signatures to get me in.

I learned how to be an infantryman at Fort Benning, Georgia, and was immediately deployed as soon as I got to my duty station in Fort Bragg, North Carolina.

First was Iraq with a couple of the guys I'd trained with.

Specialist Mack, Private First-Class Hawthorne, and I were thick as thieves, and as close as friends could be given our situation. We had the special assignment of providing security to, from, and during any meetings that transpired between our commanding officers and local nationals - guys like Sheiks and community leaders of that war-torn country.

We'd drive them out to these shacks in the middle of the desert, or to some random house in the town or village, or to a cow farmer's farm. They'd talk about bridges and hostiles, and money would change hands. Still, overall, I never got one inclination that demons were present, weaving their way into the humans' governing politics. Not once. It was as if I were there for nothing."

He paused for another breath, but I was careful not to say anything that would interrupt him.

"So, eventually, I just focused on being a good soldier, so I could go home and report that I'd found nothing.

When I wasn't out on a mission of protective detail, Mack, Hawthorne, and I would watch movies on Hawthorne's laptop, play soccer with the local kids, or work out in the makeshift gym we had on our combat outpost.

There were long days and longer nights where we'd pass the time as best we could.

Mack would tell us about the phone calls he'd gotten from his wife and kids, or show us pictures of all of them, and tell us about the life he left back home.

Hawthorne talked about this girl he left for most of that deployment, who'd promised to wait for him, but about six weeks before we were supposed to come home from that one, she sent him a Dear John letter.

So, we still ended up talking about her, but our perspectives had changed dramatically after she left him." He laughed a little darkly before he continued. "Our conversations were filled with things like, 'You're too good for her,' and, 'Think about how many options you'll have when you get home now.'"

I found myself smiling at his story until I heard the next part of it.

"We were having that very conversation when the first mortar round dropped on our post. It was so loud my ears were ringing, and honestly, I had a hard time for a second trying to remember what I was supposed to be doing in that situation.

But we ended up grabbing our weapons and finally found our positions to return fire.

I'd just sighted in on this guy crouched behind an Iraqi taxi with its trademark orange and white paint job, and a vision blasted through my mind.

I saw a room full of 'bad guys' calling the shots that day, and I'd recognized the building they were in as being one that we could see from the other side of our post. The vision had been a bit blurry, but I'd been convinced.

I got Mack's and Hawthorne's attention and told them to follow me. We ran in the opposite direction of all the other soldiers, and when we got to where I thought we should be, I pointed out our target to them.

They'd seemed confused at first but trusted me anyway, and I led them over to the machine gun point where our .50 Cal was staged for base security and racked the belt on it while they reloaded their weapons behind a T-Wall."

Adam took a few breaths then, almost as if he was having trouble telling me the rest, and I didn't know what I could do right then to make it any easier for him, so I just started rubbing his chest with my thumb.

"I lined up with the building a few hundred yards away and took aim, then started firing.

Immediately, there was return fire from the building next door to the one we were aiming at. Nothing was coming back from the target, so I shifted fire and lit up the house next door.

And after a few minutes that felt like hours, all the shooting stopped, and I started to relax.

But that's when I heard Hawthorne starting to freak out.

He'd screamed, 'Mack!' as he ran to the other side of me, and I looked right to see Mack was there bleeding out.

I didn't need to check for a pulse because I already knew he was gone. Hawthorne knew it too, but he just would not stop checking anyway.

I called in a medic and tried to get Hawthorne to calm down, but the only thing that worked was using the same tactic I would on Marcia - I just held him and let him wail into my chest."

His voice cracked some as he said, "I cried right along with him."

Tears were forming in my eyes as I listened to one of the strongest men I'd ever met in my life become emotional, and had to work really hard at not letting him know how his story affected me, for fear that he would stop talking.

"Eventually, after Hawthorne calmed down enough for me to let go of him, he puked his guts up.

After that, I tried to get us back to some semblance of normal, but Hawthorne was never that same happy go lucky guy again, and I missed the unjaded version of him so much.

He ended up turning into this cold soldier who never got close to anyone else besides me.

We went on two more short deployments together to Afghanistan.

I guess he just didn't know how to live back home, how to live without a mission, and part of me always knew he'd never be at peace again. Never feel right about being so far away from where Mack died. He had to go back if only to be closer to where he left his heart, and since the hunters hadn't come to get me, when Hawthorne said he was going back again, I knew I had to go with him.

I asked to go, and they let me eventually, but I had no idea we'd only be in country for three days when Hawthorne would get shot through the face by some kid too small to even be holding a rifle.

I'd shot back before I even saw the target."

Adam went quiet again, and I just kept up the circles I was drawing on his chest with my thumb as his hand stilled on my back.

"When I finally saw my victim's, Hawthorne's killer's small body, my mind jumped back to the family I'd inadvertently killed that day Mack died.

When we searched through the house I'd initially been targeting because of a cloudy vision, I saw all those innocent faces again. Two boys, no older than five, a little girl still in diapers, cradled lifeless in her mother's limp arms, and the father's body lying by the window, helpless to protect his family from the fifty caliber bullets I'd ended their lives with."

My insides felt like they were curling in on themselves as tears flowed from my eyes, but I was deathly still. Though he'd given me no indication, I knew that Adam needed to get everything out, and even though it was tearing me apart to listen to what he'd been through, I did it anyway because I wanted to be that person for him. I wanted to be who he could share anything and everything with, to hell with how it broke my heart.

"All of their faces plague my dreams at night, and I know there's never going to be an end to the guilt and shame I feel. It doesn't matter that I'd also killed all the bad guys in the house next door. I don't see their faces when I sleep.

I only see the ones from that innocent family, my friends' lifeless and bloodied faces, my sister's crumbled and squinched face as she crawled over to me when I busted through the door of that abandoned warehouse.

Those are the images that will haunt me for the rest of my life, the reason why I'll only talk about a vision or act on one if it's crystal clear to me, as much as it might piss off those that are around me.

Derrick and Tyler, the chief, even Brax... I just need them to wait sometimes."

His story stopped, and his chest fell, his lungs deflating as he breathed out beneath me.

I sat up then, and while my head was still facing away from him, I wiped the tears from my cheeks as best I could before I turned to look at him.

"Adam," I said sincerely, "I will never rush you to tell me what you see, I promise, and I won't let any of them do it to you either."

His smile was genuine and grateful as if he really needed to hear me say that, and as he brushed his thumb over my cheek again, I couldn't stop myself from reaching down and wrapping him up in my arms. I hugged him as tightly as I could, needing to comfort him just as much as he was comforting me by returning the hug.

"I love you, Becks," he said, the air from his breath tickling the top of my head, and as my heart swelled inside my chest, I knew through and through that I felt the same way.

"I love you too, Adam."

CHAPTER 11

BECKS

"Hey," Adam's voice startled me out of the almost asleep state I was in, and I jerked to sit up and look down at him.

"Sorry, I didn't know how tired I was," I said. "Did you say something?"

He smiled as he answered, "Don't be. The gauntlet takes so much out of you, I'd be surprised if you weren't tired. I didn't say anything, but I know you wanted to spend time with everyone, so as much as I want to hog you all to myself, I know I shouldn't."

There it was again, that selflessly sweet aspect of Adam that I just couldn't get enough of. "You're right; I do need to go," I said as I leaned down to kiss him before I scooted off his bed and started heading toward his door.

As I reached to open it, though, Adam got up as well and beat me to the door just so he could kiss me one more time before he let me be on my way.

When his door shut between us a few seconds later, I stood in the hallway, just wrapping my mind around everything that had already happened with Tyler and Adam so I could compose myself before I headed somewhere else.

I knew I was going to see Derrick next, but I wasn't entirely sure I was ready for the training or lessons he, undoubtedly, wanted to teach me. However, I didn't want to miss out on time with him, even if it was spent doing things I wasn't necessarily happy about.

I'd gotten my time with Tyler and Adam; I wasn't going to miss out on an opportunity with Derrick if I had any say in it.

Though, I thought I might be able to steer the conversation into something other than training if I played my cards right. *'If I can get him doing something he likes to do, I know it'll distract him from what he feels like he has to do,'* I thought as a plan started to develop in my mind.

Instantly, a red and black bathing suit appeared on my body out of nowhere, and I sent a thankful thought toward my power for her help. She didn't respond at all, other than by sending a warm tingling feeling through my body as if she were wrapping me in the only kind of hug she could give me. Though a part of me wondered why she wasn't talking to me like she had in Hell, I didn't give it too much thought before I was headed out to the beach.

As soon as I stepped through one of the sets of sliding glass doors, the breeze off the water had my hair flying everywhere, the air filled with the scent of saltwater, and I smiled as the sun hit my face. It was insanely bright outside, and I had no idea what time or even what day it was, but I knew I only had a short amount of time left to enjoy life the way it was; I wanted to embrace it and savor it as hard as I could for as long as possible.

Derrick was sitting at the outside table with a beer in his hand when I got there, and I didn't miss his sharp intake of breath as he saw me standing there in my bathing suit. A shiver went down my spine because of it, and it was everything I could do to just act natural and normal, instead of girling out like a crazy person.

"Going for a swim?" he asked after he cleared his throat.

"Care to join me?" I asked smoothly, cocking an eyebrow in his direction, not knowing where that sassy ass side of me came from, but I was thoroughly elated with how he responded to it.

His smile was instant, but his eyes darkened in that signature way of his that had my belly flipping. As he sat his beer down and stood up, his eyes never left mine, and even though it was hard to do, I didn't look away or blush like I knew I would if I wasn't controlling every aspect of myself.

He had that power over me, Derrick specifically, where one look from him could send shivers down every inch of my skin and heat to my cheeks.

Where Tyler was playful and forward, Adam was sweet and open. Derrick was intense and hid his feelings and thoughts from me most of the time. I was learning all of their tells, though, and I knew that when Derrick's eyes darkened like that, his mind was thinking something that had to do with me, though I hadn't quite figured out exactly what those thoughts were yet.

I did, however, plan to find out.

Derrick didn't say anything as he took his shirt off and draped it across the back of one of the chairs. He just did it and walked over to me, holding my gaze until he grabbed my hand and led me down the stairs into the sand.

His mouth was in a tight line, but after having seen that before, I knew it was because he was controlling himself, too, keeping himself from saying or doing something he otherwise would want to do or say.

I didn't know how to make him drop that control and be open with me like Adam had been. It was an almost effortless task for me to do with Adam, though.

With Adam, I really just had to listen without judgment, a feat made so much easier by the fact that I couldn't bring myself to judge almost anyone for nearly anything.

Getting Derrick to spill was much harder. I'd found myself wondering how to break him out of his 'do right' shell many times, and this was one of them.

However, right as my feet touched the water, I realized I didn't want to wait any longer to find out what he was hiding from me. I didn't want to keep having to control myself around him, nor have him do the same with me.

"Enough," the word came out of my mouth as a trailing end to my internal thoughts, but I played it off as if I'd meant to say it.

Derrick stopped and turned to look down at me, the sun lighting up his face and making his brown eyes piercing as he regarded me.

"Enough, what?" he asked, and it took me a second to gather what I wanted to say to him.

"Tell me what you're thinking. You haven't said anything since I asked you to join me, and not knowing what you want or feel or think is driving me crazy, has been driving me crazy since I met you. Like just answer me like a normal person! You can't just look at somebody like that, like you do all the time, without explaining yourself. It's too intense to not give an explanation." My words got evermore emotional as I spoke them, but I couldn't find it within me to care much since I was basically pleading for him to be honest and forthright with me.

"How do I look at you?" he asked, that same look in his eyes as he said it.

"The way you're looking at me right now!" I nearly shouted. "Like all...," I said before I mimicked him as best I could by tilting my head down, pinching my eyebrows together, and dropping my eyelids a fraction from where they sat naturally.

A laugh escaped him then, and I dropped the charade as anger settled within me. I crossed my arms over my chest and leveled him with a glare all my own as he just kept laughing at me. Still, if I was honest with myself, his laughter, whether directed at me or not, affected me. It made me want to laugh with him, but I held my ground and kept my face stern until I finally got the answers I needed.

"Please tell me that's not what I look like." His chuckles were dying off as he asked me that, and despite myself, his words had my mask cracking and a smirk forming on my face that I couldn't hold back entirely.

Standing my ground, I said, "It was an accurate representation-like the best impression of you ever made, if I do say so myself."

He started laughing again, and I couldn't not join in at that point, so for a minute, we were both just standing there laughing at each other. However, before our chuckles died off completely, he pulled me into him by my waist, putting my back to his front as he wrapped his arms around me.

The move surprised me, but his words surprised me even more.

Leaning down and whispering in my ear, he said, "I hide what I think from you because the thoughts I have aren't exactly pure. Most of the time, they are highly inappropriate, and I don't want to scare you away."

Sobering while also becoming intensely turned on, I asked, "What makes you think I'm not feeling the same way?"

I knew his playful side was gone instantly as my words hit his ears; I could feel it in the way his body felt up against mine as if he hadn't been expecting me to say that.

He took his arms from around me, only to grab my hips and turn me around to face him. His hands were planted solidly on my hips, firmly enough that I knew it would be a struggle to get out of his grasp had I wanted such a thing. I didn't.

That same intense stare was in his eyes again, but I didn't even have a chance to say anything about it before he was finally telling me what was behind that stare.

"Right now, I'm thinking about how good your hips feel in my hands." His grip tightened for emphasis. "When you walked out of the house, all I could think about was how good you look in that bathing suit." His gaze slid down the front of me, and a zap of electricity went straight through me, right to my girly parts. "And sometimes, when you open your mouth, all I can think about is what that mouth might be able to do." Subconsciously, my tongue went out to wet my lips, and his eyes watched the motion closely.

"It's very distracting. *You're* very distracting," he said, pulling me just a hint closer to him. "How am I supposed to figure out what this team is supposed to do, or give orders, or even think when you're around, huh?"

My stomach was alight with millions of butterflies, and my skin felt like it might just vibrate right off my body, but my brain and its self-deprecating filter slipped its own fears through my mind.

"Is it just my body that distracts you?" I asked without thinking about it first. I wanted to take the words back as soon as I said them, even more so when Derrick reared back like I'd slapped him.

I hadn't meant to fuck up the moment, but a huge aspect of what self-respect I did have, was based on the fact that I couldn't be just an object for anyone ever again, and call me needy, but I needed him to clarify that he didn't just want me for what my body could give him. I needed way more reassurance than that.

"No, Becks," Derrick said after he recovered from what I'd said, a stern look falling over his face again as he looked at me. "Your body is not the only thing that distracts me. Hell, everything about you does that to me. What you say; how passionate you are about what you believe in; how no matter what I say or do, you're going to do what you think is right at the time... I could go on and on about the things I love about you, Becks."

I was getting all soft and mushy from what he was saying, but all those feelings were replaced by pain when he spoke next.

"I'm not one of the monsters from your past that you need to protect yourself from, so please don't discredit what I feel for you or the kind of man I am by lumping me in with them and assuming I see you the same way as they did."

It felt like my heart had stopped in my chest as I realized that was exactly what I'd been doing, assuming the worst from him based on my shitty past. The reality was that Derrick had never given me a reason to doubt his motives or to fear him, and so my treating him like he had was remarkably dismissive of how well he actually treated me.

Before I could respond, though, his features softened, and his voice dropped lower as he said, "Yes, I want your body; I'd be a fool not to. But I want everything else about you as well. I want every piece of you

I can get… your heart, your mind… anything you're willing to give me, I'm here for it."

Dumbass tears wanted to well up in my eyes at his words, and a flash of anger went through me because of it, but when one dropped down my cheek, Derrick sent one of his thumbs up to catch it and wipe it away. Which only caused a few more to fall, despite me.

"That's really good to hear, Derrick," I said as I sent my hands up to each side of his face. "But how could you think that I don't want all that from you too?"

I could tell my question got him by the way his eyes widened some.

"You want every part of me, and I want every part of you, but you haven't been sharing any of your feelings with me; you've just been looking at me funny or avoiding saying anything. This should be a two-way street. I'll show you everything, but I need the same from you."

Derrick stared at me for a minute before he pulled me into his chest, and my face rested against his skin below his chin. "That makes sense, Becks." He took a deep breath, and I could hear the air entering his lungs. "I'll try my best to let you inside my head, and I'm sorry for keeping you out."

A small giggle escaped me, but I didn't know why. Maybe it was happiness? Relief? I had no idea.

"But can I ask a favor of you to help me with that?" he asked, and all the thoughts I'd been thinking disappeared as I looked up at him, knowing I was willing to do anything he needed me to do.

"Can you ask me when you want to know something? I know you see through me when I'm lost in my own head, but it's not easy for me to just put everything out there." He glanced at the water for a second before he turned back to me and explained further.

"You know I was raised in a very strict household where sticking to the rules was paramount. Yes, it was full of love as well, but that training, mixed with having to lead this team and the pressure of trying to prevent the apocalypse, can just feel overwhelming sometimes. Almost like I have to keep my cool all the time and make the right decisions at every turn.

I'm willing to go against all of that to let you in, but sometimes I might need you to ask me to let it out because I'm afraid it won't even cross my mind to tell you, given how I've lived up until now."

There was not one ounce of me that would refuse him if he needed it, and it would allow me to see him and know him more closely. "Absolutely, I will."

His smile was soft but genuine, and as he kissed me and my toes curled in the sand, I knew we'd made some significant progress just then - progress toward a better understanding of one another that I wouldn't trade for the world.

Pulling away after a short time, he asked, "Now, how's about that swim?" and all I could do was smile and nod before he was running into the water, guiding me by my hand right beside him.

CHAPTER 12

ABSINTHE

I was sitting there in the tree watching as Becks and Derrick frolicked in the surf, attempting to weed out just why I felt the way I did about Becks, just as I always had since her parents brought her to me sixteen years ago.

Her laugh reached my ears then, brought to me on the breeze off the ocean, and a tingling feeling erupted in my chest as I heard it.

It was like I was drawn to her for some reason I couldn't figure out, but I'd begun ignoring the incomprehensibleness of it all since there seemed to be no end to it or rhyme or reason behind it.

There was no reason in all the versions of the future I'd seen for me to feel the way I did. In every one of them, Becks was central to keeping the world spinning, but I couldn't see anything past her gauntlet.

My best guess had been that she was going to either kill me directly or end me indirectly when she passed through the gauntlet, one way or another; it was the only logical conclusion I could come to.

Eternity is a really long time, and though I didn't want my time in this realm to be over, I wanted to make sure Becks was successful, that she was alive... that she was happy.

Her well-being was all that seemed to matter to me anymore.

Ever since I changed the future through the deal I made with her parents and saw everything she was going to have to go through to become who she needed to be, her happiness had trumped even my love for myself.

I knew she would literally be the death of me somehow, but I just couldn't find it in me to begrudge her that, so long as she lived afterward.

I knew the jinn I'd been before Becks, and I wasn't afraid to admit any of my wrongdoings. I'd done so many terrible things that when the hunters, witches, and angels sentenced me to live in my cave, I knew I'd had it coming, that the world was probably better off.

Still, even that consequence hadn't silenced the drive I'd had to wreak havoc.

Nothing had until Becks came along.

I'd tried to ignore my feelings as best I could after I made the deal with her parents, just thinking that the future needed time to sort itself out after all the changes I'd made to it, but after a while, I knew there was no getting around the fact that my days were numbered.

The end would have come if I hadn't done what I did, and somehow, I'd set up my own death in the process. I think that's what started my obsession with Becks originally: the fact that I knew she would kill me.

However, as my obsession grew, and my need to explain myself to her became so overwhelming I could hardly stand it, I stopped questioning what I could do to keep myself alive and solely focused on making sure the odds weren't stacked against Becks as well.

It would've all been for nothing if I were to die and Becks wasn't able to succeed, so along the way, while she was growing up, I'd done everything I could to ensure she had the life experience she'd needed.

After I explained myself and bound myself to her, I'd thought I'd feel better, that I wouldn't be drawn to her as I'd been before. Instead, it was as if my feelings toward her had increased ten-fold.

I wanted to laugh and play with her like Derrick was doing, reach her heart like I knew Adam had, to speak to her soul as Tyler did, to understand her as Brax could. However, I also knew it was a useless endeavor. I knew nothing I did was going to change the fact that I didn't have a future with her, so I settled for watching her as the next best thing.

Sure, it may have been a little 'weird,' as people would call it now, for me to spy on her for her entire life, but I didn't mean any harm by it, and as long as I kept my mouth shut, no one would know I'd done it in the first place.

'It's not that easy,' I thought as I considered how hard it'd been to watch my words with Becks before we made our deal.

It was as if she had the power to pull my thoughts from my head by just merely being near me. I'd found myself more than willing to tell her everything she wanted to know, and still, despite how much I knew was at stake, I'd been happy about finally being able to come clean with her about most of what was going on.

'I can't tell her about my inevitable death,' I reminded myself, knowing that I could see versions of the future if I did, and in those, everything ended, including Becks, and I couldn't have that.

She would live, and the world would go on. Of that, I was sure, so long as I played my part and did everything I could to see it happen. Even if that meant forgetting myself and assuring my own destruction.

WHEN BECKS WAVED goodbye to Derrick, and he strolled away from her, heading back inside the house, I watched as she peered around the empty beach, seeming to be looking for something or someone.

Brax was on the other side of the island, doing another perimeter check to pass the time before she decided to spend her time with him. I'd seen him pass by a few times, flying low to the ground, his eyes, ever watchful and intent. However, when he'd come through the last couple of times while Becks was with Derrick, he'd shifted his perimeter to go around through the forest behind the house so they wouldn't see him.

It was an incredibly thoughtful gesture, I thought.

"Absinthe!" Becks yelled then, and though surprise washed through me, I found myself teleporting to her instantly as if she had the power to summon me on demand. I didn't mind one bit, though, as I stood before her, taking in her presence as the sun began to set behind the safe house.

"Hey," she said, a blush forming on those cute cheeks of hers.

"You called?" I asked, pretending I hadn't been watching her the entire time I'd been away from her.

Becks smiled and looked down, a habit that apparently annoyed Tyler, but I found intriguing. "Yes," she said as her eyes came back up to mine. "I want to spend some time with you now if that's okay?"

It never crossed my mind that she'd want to spend some of her precious time with me, and I could not prevent the smile on my face that followed her words.

"I would love to," I said as I rested a hand on each of her shoulders. "Are you sure, though?" I asked. "I know you don't have that much time left."

Becks nodded, staring me down with those beautiful blue eyes.

"We could stay here on the beach or go back inside..." her voice trailed off for a second, but before she was able to offer another suggestion, I heard my voice interrupt her.

"How would you like to explore the interior of the island?"

Becks seemed surprised by my suggestion but nodded anyway. I took her hand, leading her through the sand to the path that cut through the forest.

I'd found the path while trying to keep myself from spying on Becks, right after she went in to see Tyler. However, I hadn't exactly won that battle with myself because no sooner had I found the waterfall and the deep pool I was leading her to now, than I had been turning right back around, unable to stop myself from watching her.

The woods were thick, and the path narrow, as if it didn't get much use. It was very different from the forest I'd been bound to in Alaska, but the feel of it was the same. Quiet and untouched, rarely disturbed, and wonderful. I knew as soon as I left here to watch Becks in her Heaven trials, I would never be coming back, and as much as my attention was fixated on Becks, admittedly, I was also a bit saddened by knowing the inevitable.

I felt an icy chill tingle against the skin of my palm, where I was still holding Becks' hand, and when I looked back at her, I saw that she was no longer wearing her bathing suit, but had somehow changed into more proper forest-going attire. Attire that I had to pull my gaze away from.

The t-shirt and skinny jeans she was now wearing fit her perfectly, not just in shape and size, but also in personality. I knew her affinity for clothes, and the fact that her power could now help her out in that regard made me smile for her.

"Are you more comfortable now?" I asked as we continued to traipse down the path.

Stepping over a fallen log, Becks replied, "Much, thank you."

"I'm glad," I said, adding, "but you might want to keep your bathing suit in mind," as we came to the opening in the trees where the waterfall and the pool created by it was.

I heard Becks' intake of breath as her eyes traveled all around the area, and as I watched her, I noticed the little bit of sweat on her brow and the utter joy showing on her face.

Her eyes lit up just as they always did when she was presented with something magical, and I knew this place would bring that reaction from her. It was so cute, her excitement for certain things, and it stroked my ego a bit that I'd been the catalyst for her happiness right then.

"Absinthe," she said. "This is gorgeous!"

"I thought you might like it. How would you feel about jumping in?"

Her eyes lit even brighter as her outfit changed back to her bathing suit, and it was everything I could do to keep my eyes where a gentleman would. "I'd love to," she said as she started walking over to the edge of the pool, peering into its depths.

Gently, I placed my hand on her arm, saying, "Not from here," as I pointed up to the top of the waterfall. "From there."

Becks looked at me like I'd lost my mind for a second, but soon after, I saw her features change from scared to intrigued to excited within milliseconds of each other.

"How do we get up there?"

"Hold on to me," I said.

She didn't hesitate to grab onto my arm in an embrace that almost resembled a hug as I teleported us to the top of the waterfall.

I'd made us land on a rock that jutted out over the edge, and the short little gasp that Becks made had me laughing as I pulled her into my arms in a hug she returned easily.

"Are you scared?" I asked after a moment of just enjoying her touch, but she just shook her head as she pulled back from me to look down at the pool below us. "We could jump together if you'd like?"

Her eyes shot up to mine in what I thought was appreciation as she nodded.

I reached my hand out to take hers, and I could feel sweat in her palm, but I didn't mind. In fact, I was reassured she thought she could trust me to keep her safe when I was literally asking her to jump off a cliff.

"On three?" she asked, and as she counted down, I couldn't keep my eyes off of her.

When she got to three, I jumped with her, making sure I never let her go. A sharp little squeal tore through her throat as we fell, but all that did was make me smile as we both breached the water below a few seconds later.

As soon as my head came back above the water, Becks' infectious laugh met my ears again. I turned in the water to face her, a smile on my face as she wrapped her arms around my neck, surprising me.

I didn't know what to do with my hands in that moment, but without a thought, they went right to her sides, holding her just in case she needed me.

"That was awesome! Can we do it again?" she asked, and my heart melted some.

I'd do anything to keep that smile on her face.

"Sure," I said as I teleported us back up to the top, and we spent the next half hour or so going back and forth, jumping this way and that, thoroughly enjoying each other's company. At least, I knew I was enjoying hers, and if her smile and the way she was looking at me was any indication, she was enjoying mine as well.

Soon though, it was getting too dark, and I knew we wouldn't be able to see if we didn't start heading back. She seemed to notice the same thing since she said, "I think we should go now."

"Your wish is my command," I said as I teleported us back to the beach in front of the safe house, startling her because she wasn't expecting it.

When we solidified, Becks changed her clothes back into her jeans and t-shirt before sitting down in the sand and patted the spot next to her. I didn't know what she had in mind, but I was willing to follow wherever she led me.

"That was great, Absinthe, really. Thank you for showing me that place."

I nodded as I sat down and crossed my feet in front of me. "I thought you were deserving of a little fun before everything gets so heavy again," I said honestly, knowing that I was sharing too much with her already, but otherwise, not knowing how I could stop myself.

She looked at me as if she were trying to see inside my mind, but I held her gaze and sent a hand to her thigh.

She didn't pull away.

"Can I ask you a few things?" she asked a bit timidly as she sent her eyes to the surf in front of us.

"Anything."

She was quiet for a moment but soon said, "I know we don't really know each other." She paused for a second. "Well, I don't know much about you. You seem to know a great deal about me."

Despite myself, I laughed at that. "This is all true," I said with a smile.

She had a playful smirk dancing at the corner of her mouth but continued anyway. "I would very much like to change that, though."

I was confused for a moment, not understanding, but eventually, I found the words even though they hurt to say them. "I can't *not* know you, Becks. If it would please you and if it were possible, I'd erase what I know about you, but alas, it's not."

Her gaze ripped back to mine as if she couldn't understand what I was saying, but after a second, she was the one who was laughing.

"I didn't mean I don't want you to know me; I was saying I want to know you too," her voice was full of happiness and laughter, and after hearing her words, I couldn't say that I didn't feel the same way.

"What would you like to know?"

Her hand carefully slid over the top of mine, almost as if she was fearful I would take my hand back or something, but instead, I maneuvered my hand into hers, interlocking our fingers, and began rubbing the side of her wrist with my thumb.

"I want to know everything, but I don't think we have time for that," her smile had become somewhat sad, but I knew what she was talking about; I felt the same way.

"We don't have forever, no," I said, kicking myself for getting too close to admitting everything just then. "But I can try to answer whatever you want to know in the time that we do have."

"Alright," she started before she took a deep breath. "I know why you did the things you did, why you made a deal with my parents, and I've forgiven you for it because I know it's what needed to happen. What I don't know, though, is what was in it for you? What did you get out of their deal?"

I couldn't bring myself to answer right away, and she took that opportunity to elaborate further.

"I mean, I know you got out of your cave with the deal you made with me, so it's obvious what was in it for you on that one. I just want to know what was in it for you back then, with my parents."

I knew I couldn't tell her about the flashes of her eighteen-year-old face I saw that day when she was only two. I couldn't tell her about the way those images made me feel something for the first time in forever. There was no way I could mention how good it felt to feel again, how driven I'd been to do anything to keep feeling.

One can live a life without feeling anything, but it does something to the soul, something terrible. You feel hollow and empty, lost with no direction, a figment of who you used to be.

I'd been that way, living that real-life hell every day for centuries.

All the way up until her parents came to me, and with them, a flash of hope so bright I couldn't turn them away. I just couldn't.

"Woah," she asked, snapping me out of my memories. "Where'd you go just now?"

This girl was as intuitive as she was beautiful, and though I felt lost in that moment, I also felt like she was guiding me at the same time, like if I just followed her lead, everything would turn out alright.

"I do apologize," I said sincerely. "I cannot fully explain why I've done the things I've done. Some lights must always be turned off so you can see out into the darkness."

Rather than fight me on my stance like I thought she would, she breathed a heavy sigh and nodded before she looked down at our hands where they rested on her thigh. "I understand," she said. "This life seems to be full of secrets that can only be revealed at the right time. You not answering isn't the first, and most likely won't be the last."

I nodded at her, relieved.

"Can you tell me why you were in my Hell trial vision?" she asked with a hopeful tone in her voice as she looked up at me, the sun fully set now.

"I would if I had the answer," I said honestly. "The trials work on a different form of magic that I am not privy to. I know that they always carry some form of hidden meaning, but no one can ever say definitively what that meaning is."

"I guess that makes sense."

"If I had to guess though, I was present in your trial because I'm bound to you and your team, which is a relatively simple reason, but a reason nonetheless."

She nodded and was quiet for a minute, and I let her take all the time she needed, never rushing her because I was just happy she wanted to spend any time at all with me. Much less, all the time she already had. It was like a gift, her presence, her desire to be around me, and though it was hard, keeping my own feelings in check, I did so for her unquestioningly or begrudgingly.

"When we were back at your cave, you said something about the kings I would choose, that you'd ensured the lives we would all have would turn us into the people we needed to be, so we'd all have a chance at stopping the apocalypse." Without hearing it, I knew where her question was headed. "Can you tell me who my kings are supposed to be?"

I ran a hand down my face and then slid it over the top of my head. "I want to be as forthright as possible for you Becks, but you seem to only be asking the questions I'm not allowed to answer fully."

She giggled at that but asked, "Alright, well, what can you tell me about them, if anything?"

I took a second to choose my words wisely.

"I can tell you that your kings are ready for you to claim them. That when the time comes, you'll know exactly who you'll need."

"Do I know them already? Can I choose just anyone? Or do they have to be hunters? I have so many questions."

Her questions threw me off for a second, but I answered as best I could, remembering that I'd had to prepare quite a few individuals for the possibility that Becks would choose them. There were a few hunters, that demon of lust guy, a kid that went to the asylum with her, an angel she was destined to meet during her trials in Heaven, even a few random humans just in case.

Back when her parents brought Becks to me, there'd been many possibilities for who her future kings would be, so many different potential prospects, and I'd had to prepare for each of them.

"I cannot tell you if you know them or not; that is outside my field of vision. I don't know who you'll choose when the time comes." I didn't add the fact that the reason I didn't know who she was going to choose was that I wasn't going to be around to see her make that choice.

"But I can tell you that there are many to choose from, that you can have as many as you'd like, but that you will also need to make sure that you choose enough to balance out the power that you will have, which if I had to guess, is going to be a lot."

"No pressure, though, right?" she half-joked, laughing a bit.

"No, there will be no pressure from anyone when that time comes. Your power will know who you need, and I'm sure she'll tell you her thoughts on the matter."

"Hold on," she said as she turned a glare on me. "How do you know my power is a woman?" Then, seeming to think better of her question, she said, "Nevermind. I don't want to know," with a small laugh I smiled at hearing.

We sat for a little while in companionable silence, both of us staring into the water where the waves crashed before us. However, too soon, she said, "I better go find Brax now. I'm running out of time faster than I can think."

I'd been sitting there, attempting to quiet the staggering desire I felt for Becks because I knew there was no scenario where we could have any kind of future together. I was tamping down that unreasonable part of myself, the part that still foolishly held out some kind of desperate hope despite our circumstances, shoving my feelings for her deep down within me.

Once I heard her words, though, I stood quickly and offered her a hand up as a frenzied sort of anxiety started to whisper in my ear that this was possibly the last chance I'd have to be alone with her.

I knew nothing could come of it, and I had a healthy dose of uneasiness telling me that my feelings for her wouldn't be reciprocated, but once the idea popped in my head, I had to try anyway.

"Before you go, Becks. May I try something? You can hate me if you don't like it, I promise."

Nodding slowly, she said, "Okay, what is it?"

Carefully, I stepped toward her and sent one of my hands to the side of her face.

Her sharp intake of breath spurred me on, and ever so slightly, I kissed those lips I'd been dreaming about for what seemed like forever.

Her hands went to my chest and face, pulling me closer, deepening the kiss I hadn't been sure she'd want, and while I kissed her back, the passion within me growing intense, I knew for sure that I was done for. I was a goner. She ruled me completely, and even though I knew it would end me, I couldn't find it in me to care.

CHAPTER 13

BRAX

"Finally," I said as I felt the distinctive pull on my chest, indicating Becks was ready to see me. It'd been the longest day I'd had in a very long time, just flying around, waiting for Becks to spend time with everyone on her team and Absinthe before she sought me out.

I knew what she wanted, and while I would've spent every second with her if she'd let me, and even though I still had my reservations about Absinthe, I couldn't deny her what she wanted on what could possibly be her last day alive. With a grunt, I pushed those thoughts from my mind. Becks had to succeed; there was no other choice.

As I solidified in front of her, I caught a glimpse of Absinthe slinking back into the shadows where he'd been all day. I tried not to focus my attention on it too much, though. That dude was weird, enthusiastically nice, and probably evil at the same time. He might even been a bit psychotic too, but that was just my assessment.

"Hey, Brax," Becks said with a relieved sounding sigh.

I sighed as well. Seeing her and being in her presence always made our bond feel stronger. It took away that ever-present nagging pain that was always there when we were separated from each other for too long.

She was sitting in the sand with her arms wrapped around her legs in front of her. As I sat next to her, I tried to pry into her mind to see what she was thinking, but she wasn't letting me in, just as she hadn't all day. I couldn't be mad at her for that, though; she needed one-on-one time with each of the guys, and if it meant keeping me out to make her feel better, I was happy to stay out.

It didn't mean I wasn't dying to know what she was thinking, though.

"So, how was your day?" I asked with a bit of a chuckle, the question seeming far too mundane for the entire situation.

She giggled back at me before she said, "Long." Becks took a breath and looked out to the ocean. "Long, but necessary."

I nodded. "Yeah, I figured. How are you feeling?"

Her eyes drifted over to me, then back out to the ocean as another sigh passed her lips. "Like I could sleep for the foreseeable future, but also, going out of my mind with worry about tomorrow. I mean, I know I did okay in Hell. Hell, I've got the poison necklace to prove it," she laughed at herself before she sobered some.

"But what if the reason I did so well in Hell is because I'm evil? What if I get to Heaven and they're like, 'You've failed all of this, you evil shit. Now get out before we call security,' and I'm thrust from Heaven, dead immediately because I failed?"

Though I wanted to laugh at her assumption for the absolute crock of shit it was, I knew I had to keep myself in check to be what she needed right then.

"Becks, you're not evil," I started, causing her to look at me with the most worried look I'd seen her wear in a long time. "You're literally the best person I know. You're a hell of a lot better than Roland ever was, and he made it through with hardly any problems."

I was trying to be supportive, but I also wanted to give her a dose of perspective.

She didn't say anything, and I knew I had to let that thought simmer for a minute, so I just stared out at the ocean like she was until she broke the silence on her own.

"Brax," she finally said a little while later. "How am I supposed to be these people's queen? What does that even mean?

I mean, I didn't even grow up as a hunter. I grew up as a human, ignoring my powers, abandoning them like they shouldn't exist because I was told to!"

She was motioning with her hands, venting her frustrations to me with her legs crossed in front of her. "I don't know anything about these people or what I'm supposed to do. I don't know their ways or what they're going to expect or want.

Fuck, I don't even know what *I* want!"

"That's a lot to unpack," I said, making her smile despite the tear that dropped down her face. "Let's start with that last thing. What do you mean you don't know what you want?"

She turned her body so she could look straight at me, and I did the same, so we were no longer staring at the ocean, but at each other, as the moon got higher in the sky and I tried not to think about the ticking clock we were facing.

"I know I want to be successful in Heaven's trials, that I want to live, but I don't know if I want the responsibility that's going to come with being named queen! Who needs that kind of power? For that matter, who accepts someone having that much power over them? I don't even know them!"

I smiled softly as I placed one of my hands on hers, strengthening our bond in the process, hoping that little bit of umph would help her in some way. "Forget about everything else for a minute," I said. "Close your eyes, and imagine a future where you've made it through the gauntlet and have all your powers." She did as I said, closing her eyes. I ignored the fact that she did it with a huff.

"You feel incredible, like you could take on the world."

"That's the scary part, Brax!" she said as she opened her eyes back up to plead with me.

"Just go with it, please," I said, and though she sighed again, she did as I asked.

"Now, think of the fairies and pixies, of their forest and all the good you've done there, about how many more magical things exist now because of you. Magical things that had been extinct before you came along."

I saw her face soften as she considered my words, so I kept going. "Now imagine all the other creatures out there. They're all facing some sort of mini-apocalypse, and they're all in need of saving.

They're hurting right now, Becks. They're being torn apart, broken down, destroyed, killed, and all kinds of other terrible things."

Another couple of tears fell from her closed eyes, and I could feel her love for all those creatures through our bond as she thought about them.

"They need you, and you specifically, Becks.

Do you know what Queen Agatha said to Derrick about you?" I didn't pause long before I answered my own question. "She said you *saw* them. You saw them in a way no other hunter does. It's why, even as an initiate, they felt comfortable with you. They can trust you more than they have been able to trust any other hunter.

No one else can see them the way you do, Becks.

You know what they need on instinct alone. It doesn't matter what the hunters have been doing in the past. Whatever they've been doing obviously isn't working since the balance is so out of whack anyway.

They need to change, and you are that change, Becks.

Your perspective, the way you feel about things, especially all the creatures out there, is what is needed now.

It has to be you."

I paused for a breath, and Becks opened her eyes to look down at me, tears still falling silently down her cheeks.

"It doesn't matter what they expect of a queen or what previous monarchs have done in the past. What matters is that you fix what's been broken by being yourself.

Although it seems like too much responsibility and power, the fact that you care about having too much power in the first place lets me know you'll never abuse what's given to you, that you'll never take it for granted.

I know you haven't had a choice in what's happening, that you didn't ask for any of this, but life hardly ever asks us what we want, and most of the time, you've just got to play the hand you've been dealt.

I know you'll enjoy every minute of it because you're not going to be one of those leaders that leads from a distance. It's not in you to be that way.

You'll spend all of your time with the creatures you love so much, making sure they are as happy as they can be. You'll end their misery because you know what misery feels like.

That's the job, Becks, and you're the perfect person for it."

Her chin fell to her chest as sobs escaped her throat, and I held her hand tightly, so she knew I was there for her.

After a few seconds, though, she pulled me into a hug and cried into my shoulder while I patted her biceps where I could reach, hugging her right back.

She finally let me into her thoughts then, and I couldn't help myself. I cried right along with her and offered her as much comfort and understanding as I possibly could, all while she comforted me at the same time.

About an hour or so later, I had Becks smiling again, and also, it seemed, far less worried about everything else that was going on.

Adam called out the door that dinner was ready, and as she climbed the stairs, I called out over my shoulder, "Come on Absinthe!"

I would probably never like the guy, but I couldn't hate him anymore after seeing into Becks' head. I knew what she felt for him. That alone was enough for me to at least tolerate him. Now, if he ever stepped out of line, I would be there to knock some sense into him, but from what Becks thought, I didn't need to worry about that happening.

Maybe she had a skewed, misplaced, or unwarranted trust in him, in my opinion, but I wasn't going to argue with her. If she thought she needed him, I had to trust that she knew what she was doing, and though it was difficult, sitting next to him at the table, I did it anyway.

"I don't want to be the bearer of bad news, but you've only got about five hours left," Derrick said as everyone filled their plates with food. "What do you want to do with your time?"

"You couldn't just let her eat? Man, damn," Tyler said as he rolled his eyes at Derrick.

"What?" Derrick asked. "I just want to make sure the rest of her intermission goes the way she wants it to."

Tyler started to say something back to Derrick, but Becks cut both of them off with a small laugh. "Tyler, I don't mind. Derrick needs to know what's going on, or he freaks out on the inside. None of us want that, right?"

Tyler's eyebrows raised like he was surprised by Becks' assessment while Derrick himself looked a bit called out, and Adam and I tried to stifle our own giggles.

Becks' next words sobered all of us, though.

"As much as it sucks, after we eat, I really need to sleep some more if that's okay?"

Absinthe spoke up then, saying, "Of course, it's okay, right guys?"

I couldn't tell where Absinthe fit in with this group yet, and by the looks on all the guys' faces, neither could they.

"Right," Derrick said hesitantly after a beat of everyone just staring at Absinthe like they didn't know how to respond to such a simple question. As I heard all of their thoughts swirling about the jinn, Becks started laughing again, snapping us out of our thoughts.

"You guys are ridiculous," she laughed before she took another bite of her food. After a second thought, she put her fork down and gestured to Absinthe. "Look, I know this doesn't seem like the best idea, having him with us, but I know it's the right thing to do. Kind of like how the chief just knows things, I know he needs to be here."

Becks patted Absinthe on the shoulder, and immediately, Tyler's hand went to her thigh as a thick blush colored her cheeks. I heard the sexy alarm bells going off in her mind, and I backed out of her thoughts as fast as I could, so I wasn't invading on anything private as she turned her gaze to Tyler.

They stared at each other for a second, but soon enough, Becks finished her thought. "It may take some getting used to, but I really do hope you guys learn to get along." Her voice was softer that time, and I couldn't help but wonder if it was Tyler's touch that made it happen.

"I actually agree," Adam said, drawing all of our gazes. "In every vision I've had since we were in the cave where Becks was born, Absinthe has been there, on our side. I don't know what's true or what's going to happen yet, but I do know that he needs to be around while it happens, whatever it is."

Tyler and Derrick glanced at each other, and eventually, Tyler shrugged, though his left shoulder didn't raise as much as his right because he still had a hold on Becks' leg. "Whatever," he said to Absinthe, as he almost awkwardly tried to feed himself with his less dominant hand. "Just don't get in the way, and we'll be good."

The smile that lit Absinthe's face was infectious as well as hilarious, but my residual anger at him wouldn't let me crack a smile yet.

"I knew you guys would come around," the jinn said as he looked down, still smiling as he picked up another bite of food.

"Oh!" Becks said as a new thought entered her brain. "What's happening with our missions? The Mer queen? Philippa? The vampires? All that?"

Derrick finished chewing and said, "The chief has all of that being handled while you're in the gauntlet. My dads and yours are basically filling in for us right now."

Tears welled up in Becks' eyes again, but none fell. She was extremely emotional today, and I wasn't quite sure whether it was the stress of everything she was going through or something else altogether. Still, I figured if there was any day where her emotions would run amok, it would be during her intermission.

Pretty soon, dinner was over, and everything had been cleaned. However, everyone was acting weird, like they didn't want the time to be over but didn't know how to prevent the inevitable. Even Absinthe was looking for ways to clean up, though, for him, that meant moving things from one destination to another with no real reason behind it, probably just so he'd have something to do.

Finally, Becks stood at the doorway to the hallway and said, "Alright, I'm going to go lay down now." Then sending her hands together in front of her, she asked, "Would any of you care to join me?"

Immediately, the four guys were standing before her while I hovered next to her.

Becks laughed out a nervous and flattered giggle before she said, "I mean, I don't know if we'll all fit on my bed, but I'm not turning any of you away. Come on."

As she turned to head to bed, a quick look in her mind told me she had every intention of sleeping, and hardly any thoughts of a sexual nature, so I knew I was in the clear to join them.

Everyone let her get into bed and get comfortable before we all piled in beside her somewhere, making her laugh in the process. I settled for sitting on top of the headboard, spreading my wings out beside, rather than behind me, crossing my arms over my chest as I watched them all.

Each guy was touching her somewhere, and through our connection, I knew Becks was enjoying every second of their shared time together.

Pretty soon, though, sleepiness got the better of all of us.

Once each of them was asleep, and I couldn't keep my eyes open any longer, I flew down and squeezed in between Becks and Derrick, falling asleep right along with them.

However, I didn't get to enjoy a full night's rest because the sharp pang in my chest woke me back up a short time later. I shot up and looked around, barely noticing all the guys having the same reaction as I was, the gaping hole where Becks had been lying between us, the only thing I could focus on.

She was in Heaven, and her trials there had just begun.

CHAPTER 14

CHIEF OTTO

"Tethers to what?" I asked Essence team in my office while Philippa downed her third bag of blood on the floor next to me.

"To the Void," Ben said. "We don't know what created them or why, but we're pretty sure that's what Malcolm and Mandy found out; that along with there being a traitor here, obviously."

"Well, we know who that was," I said almost to myself. "What do these tethers do exactly?" I was trying to figure out how big of a threat this new development was because I'd never heard of such a thing in all my years, but the implications of what could go wrong in this scenario were baffling and terrifying.

Logan shifted in his seat, sitting forward as he answered me. "I'm not the greatest at knowing why things happen the way they do, but I do know that whatever set up these tethers to the Void is bad. Very bad."

"From what we could figure out, it seems like these tethers are being set up to act as bridges," Brandt said as my eyes went wide.

"You mean souls going back and forth between Earth and the Void?" I asked, bewildered by the prospect.

Ben nodded. "Yes, but it's not just connecting to Earth, Chief. The tethers are connected to the Veil, Heaven, and Hell as well."

I stood up and started pacing, so my body had something to do while I thought about everything. "Do you know where they're located? Could we watch one to see if anything is passing through?"

"Already two steps ahead of you, Boss," Brandt said. "We found one in the Veil, but from what we can tell, these tethers, these bridges, they're not open yet. It almost seems like they're being built to prepare for something, but aren't being used until the time is right."

As I looked at Brandt, processing what he'd said, fear, true and powerful, slid through me.

It took a minute to think over everything quickly, but none of the men before me seemed to mind waiting.

"We need to have them accounted for, and we need to station a team at each one until we know what all this is about." The guys nodded, but I realized quickly, the hunters were already spread too thin, since Tina had taken around a third of my teams.

"Do we know if Tina was involved in this?" I asked as soon as the thought sprung to my mind, but at their solemn gazes, I knew none of Essence team knew the answer to that question.

"Alright," I said. "Your team is now charged with finding every tether to the Void that exists. As you find one, call me or report back to me so I can assign a team to watch it. If it starts to look like we don't have enough teams, we'll start separating the teams out into individuals to watch them, but let's hope it doesn't get that far."

"Yes, Chief. We're on it," Ben said as they teleported out of my office right as a weird-sounding thud rapped on my door.

Sighing, I glanced over to Philippa, who'd climbed up on one of the couches to fall asleep after her stomach was full, and headed over to answer the door.

Fergus was barely able to hold all of the stuff in his hands, and I knew he'd probably kicked the door to get my attention. I took some of the things from his hands before they fell and guided him over to one of the tables, where we put down all the things he'd been carrying.

"Be careful with that," Fergus snapped, eyeing my less than delicate placement of his microscope on the table.

Ignoring his outburst, I placed my hands in my pockets and sighed. "Alright, what's all this then?"

Fergus huffed a little as if I should've been able to extrapolate what he'd come to tell me simply by seeing what he'd brought with him, but as I continued to stare him down, waiting silently, he got over that nonsense and started explaining.

Sorting everything out into neat, manageable piles of paperwork, and carefully righting a few of the slides that had fallen over in their container, Fergus said, "I know everyone was against Philippa being the cure for the infected vampires, but Chief, now I know there's no other choice."

I closed my eyes briefly as I swallowed that information, attempting to think through other possible alternatives. Fergus didn't notice since he was occupied entirely by putting a slide on his microscope and dialing it in.

"Every elder has been infected with the serum that Tina had one of her goonies create," he started as if I'd forgotten everything. I would've interrupted him to explain otherwise, but I knew that my best bet was to just stand there with Fergus, and eventually, he'd get to whatever point he was making.

"That serum was so powerful it was even preventing new vampires from being created. Since we all know that when a sire dies, so does the entire line of vampires they've made, we've been in a rush to find a cure for this infection as quickly as possible. Philippa's blood is the only thing that has been able to cure the infection, but Initiate Becks had such a problem with letting the infected vampires feed on Philippa, I did what I could to find another way.

First, we tried a duplication spell on Philippa's blood, hoping she would only have to give blood once. I went to most of our best spell-workers, asking them to duplicate her blood, but each time, this is what happened."

He backed up from the microscope so I could have a look at what he was talking about.

When I looked down into it, though, all I could see were black smudges that didn't mean anything to me. My face must have said as much because Fergus stepped over with another huff as he explained.

"Every duplication spell has failed. The magically created blood sample gets infected just as quickly as any other sample of blood we've tested.

Then I tried to see if I could reverse engineer the serum by analyzing the synthetic compound, but, and this pains me to say, whoever made this serum is smarter than I am, and no matter what I did, nothing worked."

On the table laid all kinds of slides and files, all of which probably documented every step Fergus took to find an alternative solution to saving the vampire species, but I couldn't examine all that. My eyes had found Philippa where she was sleeping soundly, and couldn't look away as I asked, "So what are we left with now, Fergus?"

He at least had the decency to clear his throat and sound remorseful when he said, "The only way we can ensure their survival is if we let them feed from her, or let her feed from them."

I had been expecting the first part of his solution but hadn't considered the second.

"Won't she get high by drinking from another vampire?"

Fergus slid his glasses up his nose with one finger as he said, "Well, yes, but her venom is just as effective as her blood. It is a reasonable alternative."

Though Fergus was one of the smartest people I'd ever met when it came to book smarts, sometimes, he surprised me with his lack of empathy. Philippa's body couldn't be older than any typical two-year-old's, and the idea of subjecting her to the high she would feel by drinking from another vampire sent a sickening shiver through me.

The horror stories I've heard about the consequences of such a thing, even with mature vampires, were enough to have me dismissing that possibility entirely.

"Alright, I'll consider what you've told me, Fergus," I said as I patted him on the back. "Thank you for telling me."

"No problem, Chief," he responded.

"Let me teleport you and all of this back to your lab, so you don't have to carry it all."

It only took a few seconds or so to get Fergus and all of his stuff back to his lab, but even that small separation from Philippa, where I knew she was alone while I was away, was enough to have my senses piqued and my anxiety growing.

Word hadn't traveled far about her yet, but I knew that as soon as it did, there would hardly ever be a time when she could really be left alone again. Anyone with a grudge to settle with the vampires would have a perfect target in Philippa since she was the first. They'd only have to kill her, and they'd end the whole species.

I was standing over her, watching her sleep and considering the kind of life she was going to have when another knock sounded.

I was having a busy night, that was for sure.

When I opened the door, Raven team was standing there looking much like Essence team had, and without a word, I motioned for them to come inside and tell me what'd happened with the assignment I'd given them. Everyone sat down and got comfortable before Chester spoke up.

"Alright, Chief, this may come as a shock, but the Mer king is dead, and the Mer queen is taking her throne back as we speak."

I blew out a relieved sigh and said, "Yes, some good news. I knew it was going to happen; I just didn't think it would happen so quickly. Was there a battle? Any lives lost?"

The men of Raven team shared a glance with one another before they looked back at me.

"There was a small battle, but that's not the real problem here, Chief," Brock said. "The problem is, the Mer queen took out the king before he was able to open all the underwater portals back up, and now, no one knows how to reverse it."

This issue, though important, just didn't carry with it the dramatic implications I'd already had to consider tonight, so I sighed in relief again as I smiled at the team before me. "That will be a simple enough fix once Rebecca is out of the gauntlet. Once she gets her powers and binds with her kings, she'll be able to fix all the portals, no matter where they are, without a spell. So, no worries."

Brock, Chester, and Liam still looked nervous, like they were afraid to tell me something.

"What is it?" I asked.

Liam cleared his throat and said, "We also went to check on the werewolf situation."

"And?" I couldn't stop myself from asking.

I knew the werewolves had been up to something, but I hadn't known what exactly. Just that their normally reclusive and quiet society was suddenly in an uproar over something.

"They're gone, Chief," Chester said, and for a second, I couldn't process or understand what he'd said.

"They've all disappeared without a trace."

PART III
HEAVEN'S TRIALS

CHAPTER 15

BECKS

*P*ain and fear seared through me again, startling me awake with the intensity of it, but where I'd been confused on my descent into Hell, this time, I knew all too well that I was headed into Heaven.

As the overwhelming feelings spread through my body, I tried to keep my mind in check, reassuring myself that this was just the crossing over that felt this way.

It was much easier to process as a thought in my mind than it was an actionable notion I could do anything about.

However, after what was probably a very short time in reality, but what felt like forever to me, I came into existence standing in a dining room full of people. However, there was only one person that I recognized.

Tina.

She was sitting at the table next to a man that I just knew had to have been her husband at one point, even though I also knew that man had been dead for a long time.

There were two highchairs, one on each end of the table, and in each of them were smaller versions of Tina and her husband. On a bench across the table sat two more children, sitting on their knees to reach the food in front of them.

'This is her family,' I thought with wide eyes, but as my power confirmed what I thought, fear for what I was being shown crawled through each of my senses.

'Yes, Becksy baby, this is the family that Tina lost.'

They all seemed so happy that I found myself smiling at the vision before me, wanting to join in with them for some reason, but again, I could not move.

Suddenly, another man crept through the doorway behind Tina silently.

I could tell just by the look on his face that he had ill intentions. As I realized what I was about to be shown, I tried like hell to stop it from happening, but my body wouldn't move, and none of the warnings I was shouting out registered to the people sitting before me.

The entire scene played out in fast forward, but I understood everything without difficulty.

I watched as that man first incapacitated Tina and her husband before he then tied them up to watch what he did next.

I heard the wails from Tina as she pleaded with the man to spare her children's lives, her husband's life, her life, but nothing she said or begged for even made the man slow down.

I saw when the light and life left each of their faces, one by one, just as Tina had.

I couldn't describe that level of shock and fear and sadness if my life depended on it. I happened to be frozen in place at the time, but I don't think I would've been able to move anyway otherwise.

Witnessing something like that... it shuts your brain down completely. Your body doesn't exist anymore; your emotions are cut off from feeling anything other than absolute horror. And for a substantial while, until your brain comes back online, you're stuck, unable to do anything.

However, when thoughts start back up again, you're so traumatized that none of the ideas flowing through your mind make any sense. It just turns out to sound like garbled and shocked nonsense, making the situation so much worse.

I hadn't even noticed my body's ability to move had come back to me after witnessing everything I'd seen until I felt my hands covering my mouth and tears running down my cheeks.

Tina had finally killed the man who'd done all this to her family, but not before he took the lives of everyone she loved, and as she knelt down, pulling her children into her arms, screaming their names in agony, a cry of my own tore through my throat as I fell to my knees beside her.

She still couldn't see or hear me, but I put my hand on her shoulder anyway because I couldn't prevent myself from doing so.

I was sitting there with her, watching, and wracking my brain to figure out what I could do when I heard a voice speak to Tina.

"How dare he," the male voice said, and I looked around in fear trying to find the source, but couldn't see anyone besides the dead bodies that surrounded us.

"How dare he murder your family simply because you have magic."

Tina didn't look up at the sound of the voice, and for a moment, I wasn't even sure she'd heard it.

"You didn't deserve this," the voice droned on, but it was Tina's next statement that had my eyes growing big as I regarded her.

"I didn't deserve this," she said, and for some reason, all I could think of was that she sounded like a robot, like she was being force-fed the words she was saying.

"It's the humans that are at fault for this," the male voice purred like it was proud of itself for coming to that conclusion.

Tina immediately spoke up after him. "The humans are to blame."

A prickling sensation traveled down my side, and as I turned my head to the right, I could see that with every word Tina spoke, some shape, some form was starting to solidify next to us.

It was blurry at first, but as the voice/apparition/form thing kept talking and kept making Tina respond like a hypnotized nutjob, the male voice started to take shape.

"You should seek revenge. You should avenge them," the voice said, and I could just barely make out the lines of his face as Tina spoke next.

"I will kill them all," Tina said, and immediately, I knew what I had to do.

I stood, using my power to bring my dagger to my hand again, and lunged at the blurry man, hoping I could stop whatever he was doing from influencing Tina. However, as my dagger slid through nothing but air and my surroundings changed, cheers erupting around me, a potent and unsaturated feeling of unfulfilled bloodlust developed inside my chest.

I knew I needed to focus on what was going on around me, to pay attention and look out for the next of Heaven's trials to begin. Still, all I could do was connect the dots of Tina's story, and with each puzzle piece drifting into place in my mind, anger became my sole trajectory.

Absinthe had mentioned he thought someone else was manipulating Tina somehow, back when we were talking outside his cave in Alaska, and my vision had just proven that as fact to me.

Tina may have been vengeful, and from my perspective, she had every right to be. At least toward the human that killed her family, but it was someone else's fault that she'd chosen to take her vendetta out on the entire world.

Whoever it was that was controlling her was the worst kind of evil in my opinion. That man, whoever he was, prayed on her when she was at her most vulnerable, had ensured she'd do his bidding simply because she was so lost to her own pain and suffering at that moment. And no matter what she chose to do after that, be it starting an apocalypse, setting in motion the course of events that led to my real parents' deaths, or trying to kill my team and me, every decision she made was probably not her own, and I had to consider that.

Tina wasn't the enemy; it was whoever or whatever that ghost man had been. He was the real reason the apocalypse was coming so soon, why everything in my life had played out the way it had, and as my next Heaven trial began, I knew beyond a shadow of a doubt that if I made it through, that thing was going to pay.

~

I RUBBED my eyes as the world around me shifted and molded, changing rapidly from Tina's old dining room to a giant white room that was so bright it hurt my eyes when I opened them.

In front of me was a curved stone table, white as well, with three angels sitting there waiting. The way they sat at the table and stared at me made me feel like I was on literal trial for something, and as the words fell from the angel's lips that was sitting on my right, I knew I was right to feel that way.

"You have killed. Not only in real life, but you've also chosen to kill during your gauntlet as well."

What he said didn't really require a response, but I found myself wanting to answer him as if it were. However, I shut my mouth as tightly as possible because I knew there was no sense in letting it run if I had no idea what it should say beforehand.

The angel on my left spoke then, her voice strong and smooth. "You have had impure thoughts, evil thoughts, your entire life. And those thoughts have rarely been balanced out with good thoughts as well."

'Well, no shit,' I thought sarcastically, still fighting the pull they had on me that was making me want to speak.

The angel sitting directly in front of me added to my list of wrongdoings by saying, "You love those closest to you more than you love those you have never met, yet each of their lives is just as real as the one you now live."

I didn't know what they wanted me to do, and a task had yet to be stated, so I just stood there as the urge to speak kept growing inside me.

"Do you deny our accusations?" the one in the center asked, and at that direct question, my mouth flew open of its own accord.

"I deny nothing. I killed my rapist because he hurt me and so he wouldn't rape again. I killed the apparitions in Hell for different reasons, but the same is true for all of them: I did what I thought was right. When given a chance to kill an innocent, I didn't, and I think that should say something for my character."

I had no idea what I was saying, even though I knew every word I said was true. It was as if I were being given a chance to lie or fib my way out of admitting what I'd done and the decisions I'd made, but I just didn't see a point in lying to them when they probably already knew what was going on anyway.

"Your honesty is appreciated," the one in the center with the big gold eyes said. "You've won this trial as well as your last."

My brain was working on overdrive, trying to logic my way through what'd happened, but my mouth spoke sooner than I'd really wanted it to. "And just how did I do that? What was the point of that first trial? Just to show me that Tina was being influenced by someone else? How is that a test for me?"

I wanted to throw my hand to my mouth, take the words back, or die of humiliation. I mean, who questions an angel that probably has the power to off me in a split second if he sneezed wrong?

The angel in the center looked at me more closely after the word vomit dripped from my tongue, and under the pressure of his gaze, I had a whole physiological reaction I couldn't quite explain.

"Queen Rebecca, that trial was meant to be enlightening, and I can tell by what you've deduced from it thus far that it was largely successful in that endeavor. However, that trial was also designed to test your ability to forgive. Which you did. You forgave Tina and turned your abilities on the true perpetrator of the crime that was committed against her."

If I thought I'd been confused before, it was nothing compared to how I felt now. The words the angel said next didn't help that fact either.

"We can see inside your heart and soul. Though you may not believe that you've forgiven Tina, the reality is that you have. You know that if she were never put in that circumstance, she would've never made all the choices she made afterward, that if she were never influenced by another, the events that unfolded would've never happened. It's that acknowledgment in your heart and soul that allowed you to win that trial."

He paused for a moment, but all I could do was stand there, attempting to process his words.

"I hope you understand now. We don't go about our trials in the same way Hell does. Where they like to thrust you into nightmares of conflict, we much prefer being straightforward and forthright about things. You may ask any question you'd like, and we will answer them to the best of our ability, so long as they don't interfere with the rest of your trials."

I was floored, and everything that brown-haired angel said just threw me for another loop. I hadn't expected that answer from him, that honesty on his part, nor the pinpoint accuracy he seemed to be able to see me with.

"We're moving on to your next trial now unless you have more questions you'd like to have answered?" he said, and despite my brain telling me to shut the hell up, words spilled from my mouth without my permission.

"Who are you?" I heard myself ask.

The angel in the center with the golden eyes, chiseled chin, and smooth black hair stood, saying, "I am Micheal. It is nice to meet you, Queen Rebecca."

He then gestured to the angel on my right, causing that angel to stand up as Micheal said, "This is Elyon."

As the third angel, the one on my left, stood, Micheal said, "And this is Sariel."

"We make up what is known as the Angel Tribunal," Sariel said, causing me to glance over at her. "I believe you've heard of us through your familiar, Brax?"

"Yes," I said, a bit meeker than I'd wanted to sound. "He mentioned you."

"On to the next trial," Micheal said as he and the other two angels sat back down like they had some kind of telepathy going on, and I tried to prepare myself for whatever it was they were going to throw at me next.

"Your first two trials in Heaven are meant to ease you into the way we run our part of the gauntlet, to transition you from what you experienced in Hell into what we will be doing here," Elyon said.

"The rest of your trials will be done right here, in this room, through a simple conversation with us. We will present you with a set of circumstances and choices. You will then respond, and we will let you know when and how you pass or fail each one. Do you understand, Queen Rebecca?" Sariel asked, and I found myself nodding in response.

"This does not mean that these trials are any less pressing or important than those you have experienced thus far. You need to understand this," Micheal said, and again, I just nodded because what else could I do right then?

"Your third test is this," Micheal started as Philippa appeared in the space before me.

She looked frozen, her eyes glazed over, her body ramrod straight and unmoving. Immediately upon seeing her that way, fear and anger slid through me, but I held my tongue because my power bucked within me, telling me to keep a lid on my feelings, that I had to play nice or I'd fail.

"This girl may only look to be two years old, but in reality, she is far older than that," Sariel said.

Elyon didn't wait a solid second before he added, "She is a vampire. The first one, to be exact."

"Her blood is connected to every vampire on Earth," Micheal continued. "If she dies, so does every other vampire in existence because she has inadvertently sired all of them."

I listened intently to what they were saying, but I couldn't seem to tear my eyes away from the little girl before me.

"We could not predict what she was to become, but we knew she was essential to the way things needed to proceed on Earth, so we assigned Brax to be her familiar."

Again, it was like my mouth and mind were separate as I heard myself ask, "How did she become the first vampire? Why did she have to live in a cave for so long? Why is she here, a part of my trial?" If I could've sewn my mouth shut, I would've probably felt better at that moment. Yes, I'd wanted to ask questions, but I wished I could think about them before asking them; however, my mouth just didn't want to listen today.

I thought it would be an angel that would speak up next, but I was wrong. It was my power that spoke to me, and as she did, the angels waited patiently as if they knew everything that was going on inside my head, and they were giving me the time I needed to process what was happening.

'Becksy baby,' my power purred. 'You don't need to worry about your questions; you're only doing what you're supposed to be doing here.'

'What do you mean?'

'While you are in the presence of the tribunal, it's as if they've given you a potion that makes you tell them everything. That's why you feel the need to speak so strongly. They can see into your mind, your heart, and your soul, and it's only through that transparency that you can be successful here,' my power explained.

'And just how do you know so much, huh? Aren't you me? I didn't know that, so, how could you?' I asked, anger still spreading through me from the whole situation.

If my power could've laughed in my head, I thought she might've. 'That's a conversation for another day, Becksy. Just know that I am wise and have your best interests in mind.'

'But are you separate from me? Like, do you have a name? One that's different from mine?' Whatever the tribunal had done to me was even making me question my own power, I realized.

There was laughter in her tone as she answered me. 'My name is Becks. I am you, and you are me. I'm instinct and premonition, motivation and ability... just trust me.'

Deciding to back burner the hell out of that entire conversation, I looked back up at Micheal, and without having to say anything, he answered the questions I'd asked as if no time or conversation had taken place.

"Philippa became the first vampire through a series of events we could've never predicted because that was..." he seemed to search his mind for the proper saying, "was above our paygrade."

"The diseases she was born with, mixed with the unusual and powerful magic that resided within Brax, combined when she was near death. When he fed her the blood and corpses of the bats that only lived in that particular cave... well, all of that created the perfect set of circumstances for a vampire to be born," Elyon said.

"What unusual power does Brax have?" I asked.

The angels all shared a look as if I were missing some obvious point, and though the smiles on their faces seemed genuine and not malicious in any way, I still felt my face get hot.

"Why, his blood being made of what it is, of course," Sariel chuckled as she talked. "Half gargoyle, half elf prince... that kind of combination has never existed before or since."

"Anyway," Micheal said before I could really process what I'd just heard. "Your trial is this: Philippa has killed many and turned them into vampires. They have become known as 'elders' because none of them remember her changing them. They were innocent, and she killed them to stay alive."

I couldn't help but notice the fact that they might've been insinuating Philippa wasn't innocent too, and it rubbed me entirely the wrong way.

"Through the actions of Tina, now the entire vampire species needs Philippa's blood to survive. They will need it directly from its source. However, that would mean allowing every vampire elder in existence to feed from her to ensure their own survival."

"Here are your choices:" Elyon said, "Allow the vampire elders to feed from her, or don't, and allow the species to die out."

Philippa already came with a whole host of questions that didn't have many answers, chief of which being the tremendous closeness I felt toward her as if she were my own sister or something. I had just been driven to protect her from the moment I met her. I loved her instantly, true love at first sight, though not the typical kind one thinks about with those words. I felt that way regardless, though.

Whatever the circumstances that led to who and what she became were irrelevant to me right then. I didn't care that she was 'diseased' or whatever. I didn't care that she'd killed to stay alive... so had I.

I did, however, care about the fact that she was basically still a baby. At least in her body, she was. I had yet to figure out how she could look like she understood things that she shouldn't have been able to, but that was a problem for a different day too.

The choice was hard, and I didn't see the right answer, no matter which I chose, but I knew I had to choose regardless.

"This trial is complete," Micheal said with a small smirk, and my mouth flew open.

"What? How? I haven't decided anything yet!" I said.

Micheal chuckled some as he said, "Yes, you did. Maybe not with your mind yet, but with your heart... the mind tends to be slower in situations like these. In your heart, you decided to save Philippa, knowing that she could create more vampires, but that if she died, they would all die with her."

'I mean, it didn't seem so manipulatively calculated as that in my head,' I thought to myself as I started feeling deflated, like they'd taken the wind right out from under my wings. *'But maybe that's a bit of narcissism on my part, wanting to tell them the answer even though they already know it? Whew, my brain is working on overtime here.'* I sighed heavily at that and watched as Philippa disappeared.

"So, did I pass that one, or was that the wrong choice for my heart to make?" I finally asked out loud.

Micheal smiled at me, and I tried to keep my face from blushing. My brain, body, heart, mind, and soul were just all kinds of discombobulated, so there was no way for me to rationalize why my body reacted that way when Micheal smiled at me.

"Yes, you passed that test," he said. "Here, we take a more utilitarian approach to things, believing that what benefits the most people or creatures is what should be done unless there are other extenuating circumstances. Though you chose Philippa mainly for selfish reasons because you didn't want to lose her or the species itself, you still chose what we value here."

My eyebrows raised, and I shook my head to dislodge all the thoughts I was having because I knew I'd never be able to sort all of them out, especially given the situation I was in.

"Trial four will now begin," Elyon said, and a sinking feeling started in my chest.

CHAPTER 16

ADAM

*T*he beach house had been intensely quiet as we all got ready to go watch Becks' Heaven trials, somber, worried looks on everyone's faces as we showered and ate breakfast as quickly as possible. I didn't need to ask Absinthe what was going through his mind or check my connection with Brax to find out what he, Derrick, and Tyler were feeling; it was written plainly in the hurried fervor of their movements, the sharp clench of their jaws, and the silence of their tongues.

It was as if we were all still under Becks' spell, and we were afraid that we'd break it if we spoke.

At least, I knew that's how I felt. I was still reeling from and reveling in the closeness Becks and I had shared. The memories of baring my soul to her and of her accepting me despite my past were inundating my every thought.

With one look at each of the men around me, I knew they were all in the same boat as me.

Soon enough, though, we were in Heaven's stadium, watching as Becks made it through her first three trials with hardly a misstep.

Though I knew I should be happy about her doing well, I also knew nothing was certain yet, nor would it be until she'd gone through each and every trial.

The secret no one tells you before you go through the gauntlet, and the secret we certainly hadn't told Becks before her trials began was that yes, passing the trials was essential and gave everyone an idea of how to classify you. Still, to make it through and become a true hunter at all, you have to pass the *same number of trials* in both Heaven and Hell. That was the vital determinant of whether an initiate was balanced or not... being equally both evil and good.

They don't even tell the initiates that grow up normally about this little make or break caveat.

To tell an initiate about this deciding factor before they go through their gauntlet is tantamount to signing their death warrant.

I'd seen it happen.

One of the kids I'd gone to the hunter academy with, Noah, was due to go through his gauntlet in a few weeks, so he'd been asking everyone he could find that had already been through for any inside information they could give him.

I'd been standing by Binaria West's main building, waiting for my appointment to be assigned my first mission, when Noah came up and started talking to a few others who were waiting for their assignments as well. I wasn't sitting with them, but they were close enough that I could hear what they were saying as I sat on the brick wall out front.

Keith, this guy that had been through his gauntlet only days before and had always had more confidence than he really should've had, jumped down from the brick wall and threw his arm around Noah's shoulders. He said, "Man, did you know the trials themselves aren't even that important, so long as you pass the same number of trials?"

He was about mid-sentence when I'd jumped down, intending to interrupt him and stop him from saying too much, but I was too late.

Noah fell to the ground instantly, dead on the spot, and Keith looked up like he had no idea what was going on.

I'd glared at him like he was the dumbest person I'd ever met in my life before I called for help, but I could see the emotions he was already feeling were going to do a lot more damage than anything I could ever say to him.

Needless to say, Keith will forever have to live with that guilt, knowing if he'd just kept his mouth shut, Noah would probably still be alive, and from last I heard, his obsession with the bottle had been his poison of choice for dealing with it.

Point being, Becks had an uphill and nearly impossible battle in front of her.

She had to pass six out of seven Heaven trials to make it through, which, from what I knew, hadn't been done since the queens and kings went through their gauntlets. Most initiates pass around three or four trials each. The five that Derrick, Tyler, and I had passed with was nearly unheard of, but not impossible.

Six though?

It was as if we were expecting perfection from one of the least trained initiates ever, and my worry for her reflected just how high the odds were that were stacked against her.

By the time she was about to face her fourth trial, none of us guys or Brax had said a word to each other since we'd woken up. We all knew what she was going to face today, and though a part of me wanted to rectify that, wanted to ease some of their worries if I could, I knew it would be a useless endeavor since I couldn't even quell my own.

I scarcely noted the new information about Tina or Philippa that had been shown through Becks' first few trials, wrapped up as I was in trying to fight off a vision that I could feel coming. There was no way I wanted to succumb to it while Becks was being tested, but as soon as her fourth trial began, I lost the battle with my vision, and instantly, I was in another place and time altogether.

"I can't hold it much longer, Becks!" Derrick screamed as I solidified next to him and let go of Tyler's shoulder.

We were standing on a steep, snowy, and rocky incline that I recognized as where the giants usually reside in the Veil. Glancing up, I saw their enormous castle where it was carved into the side of the mountain, maybe a few thousand or so yards further up.

The snow was in the full-on blizzard mode typical of what the humans would know as the Rocky Mountains in their dimension, and the sky was an eerie blue-gray whose light was diminishing by the second as the storm intensified.

Derrick had his hands out as he held open some sort of portal I'd never seen before. I knew instantly that Becks was in the black space I could see in the portal, and instinctively, I also knew that if he ran out of magic or didn't keep it open long enough for Becks to come back out, we'd lose her forever.

"What can we do?" Tyler yelled over the roar of the wind, looking just as panicked as I felt as we both rushed over to Derrick's side.

"I need more time!" I heard Becks call from somewhere deep within the portal, and my fear shot through the roof at the look on Derrick's face. I could tell without asking that he was only barely holding on as it was, and as he heard Becks' voice, I watched as he gritted his teeth, and the muscles in his neck started bulging as he gave it everything he had in him to keep the portal open.

"Come back now!" I heard myself scream into the blackness beyond the portal. "We'll find another way!"

I had no idea what I was talking about, no knowledge of what would lead us to that point, or what we were facing exactly. All I knew was that I felt like I was useless, that there was nothing I could do other than watch and hope she made it out before it was too late.

Becks didn't say anything else immediately, and dread started filling my soul.

However, a few seconds later, I saw the faint outline of her silhouette running toward us, Brax right behind her, flapping his big wings as fast as he could as they tried to make it back to us before Derrick's body gave out.

Even still, the fear I'd thought I had at that moment paled in comparison to what I felt when I realized Becks and Brax were being chased, followed by swirling and snarling, grotesque looking black smoky beings.

"Hurry up before those things catch you!" Tyler yelled at Becks as she got closer, but her words threw me off when she spoke next.

Jumping through the portal, she said, "Close it! Close it now!" But as she rolled through the snow in a graceless landing, I realized her warning had come too late.

Those beings hadn't been trying to catch Becks and Brax.

They were looking to escape with them.

Derrick fell to the ground, unconscious as the beings started pouring through the portal in a swarm of black and silver vapor so thick, I couldn't see through it. I didn't know why the portal didn't close when Derrick fell, but it didn't, and the only reasonable thing I could come up with to explain why was that so many of those things were passing through that it simply wasn't able to close.

They gushed through in overwhelming numbers, some of them attacking us where we stood while the rest floated up into the sky like a disturbing black and silver cloud of teeth and fangs.

They were crawling all over me and everyone else on my team, and as I fell to my knees, swiping blindly through the onslaught, I knew I didn't stand a chance. I didn't even have a moment to grab my weapon; they were on me so fast.

As I fell to the ground, my last few breaths wheezing in and out of my chest, the sight I saw as my face hit the snow-covered rocks beneath me told me no one stood a chance. Not anymore.

I'd been under the impression that this was the only portal being bum-rushed by those things, but as I glanced across the sky before me from my vantage point on the mountain, I saw three more stacks of the beings floating up in the air in the distance from other portals, looking like the choking smoke that disperses from giant smokestacks.

As the beings sucked the life out of me where they feasted on my flesh, and my lungs breathed their last breath of crisp mountain air, black and silver vapor started to engulf everything I could see in the white-out blizzard surrounding us, and I just knew this would be the end of everything.

Blackness crept into my mind before the bright white of Heaven's stadium tore through the backs of my eyelids, shocking my eyes open and forcing me to pull a chest full of air into my lungs.

I was sitting in my seat just as I'd been before the vision took me, but even though I could see Becks was still talking with the Angel Tribunal, it was Derrick's and Tyler's eyes on me that surprised me.

They each had a hand on one of my shoulders, and the looks on their faces told me they were genuinely concerned about what I'd seen. However, no sooner had I registered their troubling worry than I was thrust into yet another vision.

"Don't do that to yourself," I heard myself say as I laid a gentle hand on Becks' tear-stained face. *"Don't ever give Rick the benefit of saying, 'Well, at least he didn't blank...' What he did was wrong enough, and just because it wasn't worse doesn't mean that what he did to you was any less traumatizing or that it can be excused in any way."*

We were lying in a bed somewhere, but I didn't recognize the room. Cloudy, early afternoon light and the peaceful sound of rain dropping on the roof gave the atmosphere a magical feel like time was suspended for that moment. The lights were off in the room, and though I didn't know where everyone else was, I knew Becks and I were alone and that I was thoroughly enjoying that aspect, regardless of the subject we were talking about.

Becks looked up at me, and I took in her face, her messy bed head, her essence, and my heart stuttered inside my chest. She was perfect.

Her hand slid, first to my stomach, then up my chest as she stared into my eyes, her movements slow and controlled but tantalizingly sweet.

"How do you always know exactly what I need to hear, huh?" she asked, a small smile spreading across her face as I breathed in her scent.

Leaning forward, I felt my lips touch hers in response, but all too quickly, I was sent back into reality.

Derrick was standing right in front of me, between me and the railing in front of our seats, when my eyes opened. He was facing my left and taking up way too much of my personal space, but as I glanced up at him, I knew something was wrong by the way he was acting.

Sending my gaze to whatever he was staring at, I realized Tyler had shifted into his wolf form, right there in the stadium for some reason. He was growling toward the center of the arena, where Becks stood oblivious to all of us in the stands.

There was commotion everywhere and quite a few angry outbursts from the angels and hunters surrounding us as they all took in the sight of Tyler's wolf as well, but I couldn't pay them any mind as I looked at Tyler.

Instantly, I knew if I didn't do something, he was going to charge toward Becks, and though I had no idea what the consequences of that action would be, with her life on the line, I wasn't willing to wait around and find out either.

I stood quickly, pushing past Derrick to stand with Absinthe right in front of Tyler, blocking him from getting to Becks. Absinthe was trying to get Tyler to calm down, but he was going about it all wrong.

Apparently, Absinthe was just all smiles, no matter the situation. However, right then, Tyler didn't need jovial encouragement to get him to calm down; he needed a firm hand from someone he trusted, and since I was the only one other than Becks in attendance that could fill that role, I stepped up and did what had to be done.

"Tyler," I said as I grabbed the wolf around his snout with both hands, forcing him to look at me. "You're in there, I know it. Fight him off, tell him to back down. This is not the time or the place for him right now."

His bright green eyes strengthened their resolve at my words, and I knew I wasn't getting through to him that way. I needed to try something more direct.

"Ralto," I said warningly as he tried to rip his mouth from my hands, but I wasn't letting him go anywhere. "Do you want to get her killed?"

Instantly, I felt him back down as he considered what I'd said, and a few moments later, Tyler shifted back into his human form, looking thoroughly exhausted with sweat seeping down his brow.

"Thanks, man," he said as he fell back into his seat with a huff. "I don't know what's gotten into him."

"That's the second time you've shifted in a matter of minutes!" Brax said from the other side of Absinthe, drawing my attention to him. "What the hell is going on with you two?"

It took me a second to realize that he was speaking to both Tyler and me, but as yet another vision started to take shape in my mind, I knew what he was talking about.

Our powers were going nuts.

CHAPTER 17

BRAX

I knew when I took on the guys and accepted them as compatible members on Becks' team that there were going to be times where I'd feel spread too thin, times when I'd have difficulty doing my job being a familiar to all of them, but this took the fucking cake.

All I wanted to do was watch Becks and support her, doing whatever I could to ensure she made it through the gauntlet, even though I knew there wasn't much I could do other than watch to see what happened.

However, that's just not how things were going down.

At first, everything seemed to be going well, but then, with increasing intensity and occurrence, the guys' powers were making a scene when it was absolutely not the right time for them to do so.

Adam's visions had been the first thing to go astray, sucking him in and causing his entire body to go rigid. Though I couldn't see what he was seeing, I knew whatever he was witnessing was intense from the way his body seized up.

Next, it was Tyler. First, he shifted into an eagle out of nowhere, squawking loudly as he changed, scaring the ever-loving bejeezus out of me as I looked to my left to see him sitting there, feathers ruffled, looking like he'd startled himself just as much as he'd scared me.

The change only lasted a few seconds, and when Tyler shifted back, he looked utterly confused as he'd said, "What the fuck?"

We all just stared at him for a second but didn't press him for answers because Adam was still lost in his vision, and Becks was still going through her trials.

However, not even a full minute later, Tyler shifted again, but into his wolf form this time, taking up entirely too much space with how remarkably out of place he was, this big ass white wolf in the stands of Heaven's stadium.

When Adam finally came out of his second vision and talked Tyler back into existence, I was just as confused as they all seemed to be, but as Adam fell into a third vision, I was almost at my wit's end.

Tyler shifted again without warning into his dragon form, landing on too many angels and hunters to count, and it was right then when I really started to regret letting each of them be on Becks' team.

They were losing their minds, and I had no idea how to prevent or fix it, or even what was causing it all in the first place.

One surly angel flew over to us, where Derrick, Absinthe, and I were all standing there lost as to what we were supposed to do, and said, "You need to control this one, or you will all be asked to leave. Have some respect."

Well, that was not at all what he needed to say to Derrick right then.

Without warning, Derrick's hands flew up, shooting power at the angel with the stick up his ass, which sent the angel tumbling down the stairs and into the arena.

One look at Derrick's face told me he had no control over that outburst but that he didn't entirely regret it.

Tyler's dragon didn't seem to like what the angel had said either, and roared over all of us before he sent his big head down toward where the angel had fallen and took a deep breath.

I knew he was about to breathe fire down on the angel, but as soon as the thought entered my mind, I saw Absinthe reach up and stroke Tyler's scaly belly, drawing the dragon's attention away from the angel and down to him.

I didn't think Tyler would do anything directly to Absinthe. However, I realized I couldn't have been more wrong as a big scaley paw basically backhanded Absinthe, making him slide painfully across a few rows of seats before he fell down in between them where I couldn't see him.

It was only then I noticed most of the stands had been cleared as angels and hunters alike ran for the exits to get away from us.

Absinthe popped back up, looking down at himself like he couldn't understand what he was feeling, and as he raised his face to look at me, I saw the blood dripping from his nose and sliding down the side of his neck from his ear.

He climbed over all the seats, coming back to where we were, and as he reached us, he asked, "How am I bleeding?" like he'd never experienced such a thing.

Tyler fell in between the rail and the first row of seats as he shifted back into his human form again. Derrick sent his hands through his hair as his wide eyes looked to all of us, and Adam shot up out of the seat he'd fallen into when his last vision took him, seeming like he couldn't understand what all was going on either.

We were all just kind of standing there waiting for the other shoe to drop when I heard Michael say, "You've passed the gauntlet, Queen Rebecca. Congratulations. Please come up here and accept this gift we'd like to give you."

"Pixie titties, I missed it?!" I screamed, throwing my arms out to the sides and then through my hair like Derrick had just done as outrage flowed through me. "What the ever titty-loving fuck?" I said as I felt myself turn to stone and fall to the floor with a sickening thud.

CHAPTER 18

TYLER

"Control yourselves!" Becks said vehemently over her shoulder in our direction, the alpha order spilling from her lips as her power glowed purple, her eyes narrowing in on us from where she stood in the center of the arena.

She was able to see us again because she'd completed all of her trials by that point. However, none of us had seen the last of her tests because something was up with our magic.

I had no idea what had been causing all the chaos within us over Becks' last few trials.

It felt like I was completely out of control of my own body, and what was weird was that Ralto felt the same way. One of us was always in control, no matter what shape we took, but something was going on that made staying in any form tougher by the second. The feeling had started out slowly but intensely, and only seemed to get worse until Becks' power silenced mine and everyone else's on our team.

However, once Becks called us out, it was as if my body relaxed, and my beast went right to sleep. It was a welcome relief from the havoc I was feeling, but I was instantly embarrassed by what'd happened and the spectacle we'd made of ourselves.

Brax immediately turned back into his usual self, floating up into the air with a huff of frustration, but quickly focused all of his attention on Becks as she walked up to the center of the stone table where the three angels stood, waiting patiently.

Michael smiled down at Becks, and my beast woke up as I took in the intense way the archangel was looking at her appreciatively, but I was able to stifle his reaction quickly.

"Queen Rebecca," Michael said. "In your first Heaven trial, you forgave Tina, knowing she was more of a victim than most would give her credit for. In your second, you were honest about the decisions you've made and your reasoning behind them. Saving Philippa is what allowed you to win your third."

I watched the back of Becks' head as she nodded at him.

"For your fourth trial," Michael continued, "you proved that you are loyal to your teammates despite the wrongs they've done or the evil that resides within them. In your fifth, you showed that you are self-sacrificing and will put your own needs aside so that others may have a chance at life."

I'd missed all of that, but I planned to question the hell out of Becks soon so I could know what happened while I was otherwise occupied.

Elyon spoke next, saying, "You proved that you are humble in your sixth trial when you wouldn't take more credit than you deserve."

I may not have seen that trial, but I already knew that about Becks' character, and some part of me enjoyed the fact that others were seeing all of her traits as well.

Sariel finished the recap by saying, "You failed your last trial, though. The fact that you would let the entire world burn before you would allow harm to come to Brax is not the kind of thing we value here, but be that as it may, that choice is what ensures your success in the gauntlet overall."

Tremendous pride and happiness spread through me as I finally let myself accept the fact that she'd actually made it through, and as Derrick put his arm around my shoulders, a high-spirited laugh falling from his lips, I couldn't find it in me to resent him for it.

We'd all been so worried before, so distraught over how seemingly impossible it was going to be for her to win, that once it was over, I almost didn't know what to do with myself; I was so relieved.

"Such a fine performance deserves to be rewarded, Queen Rebecca. It's not every day that someone passes six out of seven trials here.

Please accept this gift from us, and know that when the times come that good needs to triumph over evil, this will be there to help you see it through. Take it, and may the good within you never be surmounted by the evil inside, only matched."

A white bow appeared in Becks' hands then, and a quiver of color-fully fletched arrows took shape over her right shoulder.

Gifts were given to those initiates that did well in their trials; hell, even I'd won a dagger from Heaven, but I'd never seen gifts as extravagant and powerful as those that Becks had won. Honestly, I'd never even heard of such gifts being given out, but hope manifested inside me because their arrival meant Becks was going to use them at some point before time ran out. This meant more time before the apocalypse came, more time with her, and as I celebrated the delight of that epiphany within myself, for a moment, everything seemed like it was going to be okay.

"There are seven kinds of arrows in your quiver, and each of them does something different: restoration, prevention, dissuasion, apathy, doubt, sight, and healing. You'll never need to replace the arrows you use because they will regenerate on their own, as well as disappear when they've hit their target; they know what they need to do. Trust in your bow and arrows, and they will never fail you."

I couldn't see Becks' face since I was standing behind her, but something slid through my consciousness from my connection to Brax that told me she felt pretty overwhelmed just then. It made me want to run to her, pick her up, and twirl her around... to celebrate her tremendous accomplishment, but I knew I had to keep all of that in check until the time was right.

"Now please," Michael said then with a loving smile on his face, "head back and become the hunter you were always meant to become."

Without delay, the angels of the Tribunal disappeared, and Becks turned around to face us slowly, a couple of tears seeping down her cheeks as she looked up at us.

That was our cue, and none of us missed it. All five of us rushed down the stairs toward her. Even though I wanted to, I never even gloated about getting to her first as I wrapped her up in my arms and squeezed her body to me tightly.

There was only one more step she had to take before she was a true hunter, and I, for one, could not wait for that moment to come.

CHAPTER 19

BECKS

The next few hours passed by in a flurry of commotion as the stage was set for me to finally 'become a true hunter and be shown to the organization,' as everyone kept saying.

Apparently, just going through the gauntlet wasn't good enough; I had to drink something in front of a whole lot of people to get the rest of my powers, or so I had discerned from the non-answer-answers I'd been getting from everyone.

No one would tell me any specifics, nor would they elaborate on anything, but from what I could gather, this whole thing was going to be a big deal to a lot of people, though I had no earthly idea why.

'Doesn't this kind of thing happen all the time? I'd hate to think they go through all this trouble for every initiate that makes it through their gauntlet,' I thought to myself.

I'd been taken back to Binaria West and put in a small room on the first floor where there were already two people waiting for me. Brax dropped me off after introducing me to Sierra and Aldo, saying only that he'd be back when he got done with whatever it was he had to do.

I had no idea where the rest of my team and Absinthe were or what they were doing either.

Sierra and Aldo were outrageously nice and were obviously tasked with beautifying me for some ungodly reason, but other than telling me what they were doing as they were doing it, they didn't speak much.

This meant my mind had been free to wander uninterrupted, which was actually a good thing after everything that'd happened in my trials.

It'd seemed like every time the angels presented me with a different set of circumstances, they'd just as quickly known how I felt about it, thus giving them the insight they needed to determine if I'd won or lost.

Though all the trials sucked in one way or another, a few from Heaven were the ones I found myself thinking about the most.

During the fourth trial, the angels showed me in great detail the shortcomings of my guys and Brax, as if seeing their flaws or sins or troubled pasts would somehow change how I felt about them.

Adam, during his army days, and the depths of his own guilt...

Derrick's fights with Tyler, his need for control...

Tyler, and the struggles he's had with his beast, as well as his bottomless pit of ignored emotions...

I was shown their gauntlets and their lives, and each of them had apparently made decisions that, at the outset, might've seemed heartless or cruel or irrational, but I had no context to understand them fully, so there was no way I could've judged them.

They'd shown me Brax, too, and his tendency to turn to alcohol.

However, what they thought I would miss was the fact that in every one of those instances where Brax had drunk himself into a stupor, I had been in the background, driving him to make that choice. Either by not seeing him when he was trying to get my attention, or trying to hurt myself, or any time after that night with Rick...

They'd even shown me glimpses of Absinthe's past and some of the seemingly terrible deals he'd made throughout his very long life.

However, I won that trial because I didn't judge any of them for the decisions they'd made in the past. When the angels asked me to join another team instead – one that didn't have as many skeletons in their closets, I'd remained loyal to Brax and my team, which was apparently what they'd wanted me to do.

"I'm going to start on your makeup now. Is that okay?" Sierra asked, snapping me out of my thoughts for a second.

I nodded but didn't say anything as she began dabbing my face with a sponge before my thoughts wandered right back to where they'd left off in my trials.

In my fifth test, my emotions had nearly gotten the better of me because Ava had been there. Well, an apparition of her was there, at least.

Since the night I'd left the only friend I'd ever had, I'd been trying my hardest to forget about her, to put that part of my past behind me, but I'd been failing miserably in that regard, even with all of the chaos that was my life now.

Still, when I saw her in front of me, strapped to a chair, being tortured by demons who were demanding she tell them where I was, I couldn't fight off the overwhelming emotions I felt as I looked at her face.

There was never going to be an instance where I would just stay quiet and let her suffer to protect me, not ever. It was why I'd left her in the first place, so she wouldn't get wrapped up in my life and possibly experience exactly what the angels were showing me.

As soon as that thought had entered my mind, the angels had declared my victory, spouting something about self-sacrifice or whatever, but as tears slid down my face, all I'd been able to think about right then had been Ava.

SHAKING myself out of those thoughts and the pain I felt that threatened to send tears through my freshly applied mascara, again, I noticed that the room I was in felt entirely too quiet.

All the awkward silences were uncomfortable, and I found my leg bouncing with anxiety multiple times, but I didn't know what to say to break the tension filling the room as they plucked, tweezed, brushed, and just altogether messed with me.

'Like what was wrong with what I was wearing? Why can't my hair just stay down like it always does?' I questioned in my mind.

Right away, my power answered, *'Becks, you should really just go with it. All the hoopla is for everyone else more than it is for you anyway, but if you'd relax some, you might even enjoy it too. It's not as if you've ever really been pampered or looked after like this before.'*

Later, as I stared in the mirror at Sierra's and Aldo's finished product, I had to admit, I'd never once felt as fierce or as beautiful as I did right then.

My makeup made me look flawless and had my blue eyes popping in a way I'd never thought they could. It was a little unnerving, but as I took in the rest of my appearance, a slow smile formed on my face as nervousness fell away to humble pride.

A silk, light blue, racerback tank top draped down perfectly from my shoulders, over my breasts, and stopped right at my hips, where black leather shorts gripped and hugged my body in a way that was both tight and flattering. I'd never considered my body to be an asset, but as I turned a little to see everything, I thought, *'Well, that's not half bad.'*

I'd thought the boots I'd bought at the mall the night I'd killed Rick were awesome, but they might as well have been Crocs compared to the badass boots I now wore since they made my calves look like I didn't have any aversion to exercise whatsoever.

My hair had been braided multiple times at the front in a weird kind of design I'd never seen, then gathered together and pulled back into a thick ponytail that hung down my back. Any hair that didn't grow on my head had been ripped from my body, and my fingernails had been shaped for the first time in my life.

Overall, I was pleased even though I still couldn't understand what the big deal was.

"Oh! Your weapons!" Sierra said with barely veiled excitement as she rushed over to the table where I'd laid all my stuff down when I'd come in.

With a bouncy kind of enthusiasm, she wrapped the utility belt Derrick had given me lower on my hips than I would have, and I had to assume it was because the angle of the belt was now somehow accentuating my *assets*.

Aldo stepped up and sheathed the dagger Adam had given me on my right hip, then slid the quiver I'd just earned from Heaven over my head, the intricate strap resting on my right shoulder while my quiver of arrows laid against my back. He draped my bow over me in the same way, and then Sierra placed Hell's necklace of potions around my neck.

When everything was in place, I had to admit, even without having whatever the rest of my powers turned out to be, I knew I wouldn't want to fuck with the chick that looked back at me in the mirror. She was a badass through and through, and though my emotions didn't feel quite that confident, I knew I at least looked the part I was supposed to be playing.

'Fake it till you make it, Boo,' my power said, causing a laugh to bubble up from inside my chest.

Right then, the doors swung open, and my guys stepped through with Brax leading the way.

They all stopped across the room from me as their eyes drifted down my frame in unison, but I couldn't tell if their gazes were appreciative or surprised or what, and not knowing what they thought when they looked at me had my nerves skyrocketing again.

"It's time, Becks," Brax said with a grin as tears filled his eyes.

Not knowing what else to do or say, I just nodded at him and started walking toward him.

Adam, Derrick, Tyler, and Absinthe made a path between them for Brax and me to travel through, and they followed right behind us without a word as Brax led me to whatever my future still held.

'BRAX,' I thought toward my familiar. *'Can you give me something here? Anything will help at this point. I'm so nervous, but I don't even know what I'm nervous for!'*

We were walking down the long hallway to what I knew would lead to the back of the building, but with every step I took, fear for what was about to happen slid through me in waves.

'Don't worry, Becks,' Brax thought-answered me. *'The chief will explain everything when you get outside, I promise.'*

'But why am I all dressed up, and why does anyone care that I've passed the gauntlet anyway? I mean, no one even knows who I am, right? I'm like the hunters' little secret that hardly anyone knows exists.'

Brax laughed out loud at my thoughts but answered with his mind anyway.

'That may have been true before, Becks, but now? After that showing in the gauntlet? I doubt there's a hunter in existence that hasn't already heard your name and wants to meet you. Especially after the chief names you queen tonight.'

My steps faltered, and I held my breath unintentionally as I tried to wrap my mind around what he'd just thought, but it was useless.

My face was suddenly on fire. My skin was tingling all over, and my heart felt like it was beating as fast as a hummingbird's wings. Chills spread over every inch of me, and a cold sweat broke out everywhere, but as I tried like hell, unsuccessfully, to pull air into my lungs, my fear only grew.

I knew the signs; I'd experienced them before.

It was a full-on panic attack, and there was nothing I could do to stop it at that point. It was going to consume me until it'd run its course, or I figured out how to think through it, which right then didn't seem even remotely possible.

The situation was only made worse because my power didn't seem to understand what the threat was to me exactly, and in turn, jumped into position to defend me against anything that happened.

She/I/it didn't know that I was the threat to myself right then, so as Brax turned around and came back to me, worry written all over his face, I saw my power lash out at him, sending him flying back down the hall away from me.

I knew what was happening in my head, but my power was in one hundred percent protection mode, and my thoughts weren't forming clearly enough for me to tell my power to back down.

Absinthe reached out to me then, lightly pressing his hand to my cheek, but with the panic seizing me, and with how every nerve ending already felt like it was experiencing too much to handle, his touch didn't feel light at all. It felt like a slap to my face, and my power attacked him too.

A purple orb dislodged itself from my chest to go straight into his, and as he fell to his knees before me, for some reason, I could only think about the jingly sound his armor made with the jolt.

"Becks," Derrick nearly screamed, getting my attention before he dished out an alpha order. "Calm down, right now."

Instantly, air started to fill my lungs again, my face began to cool, and my heart started to slow its incessant beating.

The relief that started seeping through me had me dropping to my knees right along with Absinthe, but as I looked into his face, my relief started receding just as quickly as it'd formed.

"Don't worry about me, Becks," Absinthe said with a fake ass smile that I knew was meant to shield me from worrying about him.

"But, you're bleeding!" I said as I reached out to wipe the blood from his face, but he stopped me before my hand could reach him.

His smile became genuine then as he said, "Uh uh uh, you can't get my blood all over you right now. You've got a title to earn." Where his hand held mine in the space between us, he started rubbing the back of my wrist in a soothing motion that had me calming down despite myself. "You look perfect, by the way."

My eyes raced back up to meet his, and the expression on his face didn't hold an ounce of dishonesty.

"Becks," Brax said as he flew back over to me, and upon seeing him, worry slid through me again.

Standing up, I said, "Oh my god, are you okay? I'm so sorry, Brax," as I sent my hands to his shoulders so I could look him over.

"I'm fine, I promise," he said dismissively with a small gravelly chuckle, then pointed one of his little hands in Absinthe's direction, where the jinn in question was making his way to his feet. "So is that one."

I didn't entirely believe him, but I nodded at him anyway.

"I shouldn't have dropped all that on you like that. So out of nowhere, I mean. I'm sorry," Brax said, his sandy-colored eyes staring deep into mine. "But the reality is that this is what's about to happen, and there's nothing any one of us can do to prevent it. You're going to get the rest of your powers and be named queen as soon as you step out those doors."

His tone was almost pleading, and I knew why once he opened his mind to me so I could read his thoughts.

Brax knew I didn't necessarily want to be queen because the entire prospect of such a thing scared the hell out of me, but he also knew I didn't have any other choice right then, that the *world* didn't have any other choice.

He didn't want to be so direct about it, but he also knew the best way to go about things was always to just rip the bandaid off, so to speak.

We stood in silence for a bit, talking through our connection while the rest of my team and Absinthe stood by, waiting patiently for us to handle what we needed to deal with.

In some ways, Brax made me feel like everything was going to be okay, that there was a silver lining somewhere in all this, but in others, the inescapable outcome I knew I couldn't avoid had panic trying to tear through me all over again.

Derrick stepped up after a few minutes and placed a hand on my shoulder, a sympathetic expression on his face as he looked down at me. "You need to get out there now, or someone is going to come to try and find you."

Taking a deep breath, I nodded at him and then looked at the door at the end of the hallway as if it were the heaviest burden I'd ever been asked to lift.

Suddenly, hands were fidgeting about all over me as my guys

shifted my clothes and weapons back into place from where they'd moved during my panic. I couldn't find it in me to mind, though, and all too soon, they obviously deemed me ready since they stepped back, looking to me for some kind of indication that I was prepared to face whatever was behind the door.

It took me a few terror-filled seconds, but soon enough, I found the courage to square my shoulders, lift my chin slightly, and narrow my gaze on where I needed to go.

The guys formed a line in front of me, Brax taking the lead, followed closely by Derrick, Adam, Tyler, and then Absinthe, as he pushed through the doors and into the early evening of what I couldn't help but feel was the last night of my life as I knew it.

CHAPTER 20

BECKS

*A*pparently, there was a gigantic arena behind the southwest wing of Binaria West's headquarters. As we walked and Brax flew in a silent line toward it, pictures I'd seen of the colosseum in Rome sprung to the forefront of my mind, apprehension and a sense of foreboding growing inside me with every step I took. This arena was made from dark carved stone, but in nearly the same design as the one in Rome, and the closer we got, the more my unease grew.

The stands seemed to be filled with people and creatures, and though I felt remarkably out of my element and at my wit's end with worry, it was beyond apparent that there was no turning back now.

My team led me through the archway into the arena, and as soon as we all stepped out where everyone could see us, murmurs, cheers, and a few outright screams reached my ears.

I couldn't focus on that, though.

If I did, I knew I'd either freeze up or run away altogether, so instead, I kept my gaze on Absinthe's back and followed my team up the stairs to the stage that had been erected in the center of the arena.

The chief was standing in the middle of the stage. I made eye contact with him as he motioned me over to stand beside him, while Brax and the rest of my team moved to stand off to the side near the edge of the stage.

"Just relax, Rebecca," Otto said softly so only I would hear him. "I know this might be a bit startling, but I'll be with you every step of the way, okay?"

I couldn't find my ability to speak right then, so I just nodded as he continued to try and ease my worry.

"When I give Marco there the signal," he pointed conspiratorially to a man that was standing down on the ground beside the stage, watching us intently, "He will amplify our voices so everyone can hear us, but I won't start until you tell me you're ready."

Somehow, I found the ability to form words again. "Well, I'm already dressed up and here, so I guess I'm as ready as I'll ever be."

The chief chuckled at that and said, "There's no reason to worry, I promise. Just be yourself, forget that anyone is watching, and I'll lead you through the rest, okay?"

I nodded at him again since I didn't have any better options, and he said, "Alright, let's get started then."

Stepping away from me, Otto nodded down to Marco and immediately began addressing the crowd.

"Good evening, hunters, and thank you for being here."

His voice had changed into what was obviously the one he used when speaking publicly, and as his voice rang out through the arena, the cheers became deafeningly loud.

I was obviously in the presence of a lot of proud hunters, and though I'd known I was joining an organization, somehow, I hadn't quite pictured them like this. I'd kind of gotten the feeling that they were all separate from one another in some way, probably because in all my experiences with Dragon team, we'd hardly ever interacted with any other teams.

However, there was no doubt in my mind they were a united front as I stood before all of them. At least the ones in attendance, that was. Tina had taken a significant number of hunters with her when she'd gone rogue, but I couldn't see one ounce of animosity in the crowd surrounding me.

"I'd like to personally say thank you to the hunters from Binaria East who've joined us for tonight's events as well," the chief's voice resounded through the space again, causing another section of the arena to applaud and cheer. "What happens here tonight will affect all of us, and I'm so glad you all made it."

'So, I'm not just looking at Binaria West's hunters here?' I thought-asked Brax as I kept my eyes on the chief and my face impassive.

My elf-goyle familiar didn't hesitate to answer me right away. *'No, you're looking at every hunter that could make it from both Binaria West and Binaria East. The chief has been working nonstop since he left your Hell trials to put this together, and even sent out a mandatory call for all hunters worldwide to come if they were able.'*

Though I cataloged the information in my brain, I tried not to let the overwhelm I was feeling show on my face.

"There is someone I'd like you all to meet," the chief said, and the cheers began to die down so they could hear him. Stepping back and sending a hand out to indicate me, he said, "This is Rebecca Mason, the newest member of Dragon team."

There was a little applause at that, but the chief continued on undeterred.

"She won six out of seven trials in both Heaven and Hell as part of her gauntlet, and..." his words died on his lips as the cheers grew again.

Heat flooded my cheeks, and I had to fight the overwhelming urge I had to run out the way I'd come in, but after a minute, even that round of cheers died down so the chief could speak again.

"And during her gauntlet, it was confirmed that she is meant to become our next queen."

The arena became deathly silent, and if I'd thought I wanted to run away before, it was nothing compared to what I felt now under their scrutiny.

I could feel everyone's eyes on me, taking me in, judging me, sizing me up, but it was Brax's thoughts that cemented me to my spot and had my chin lifting slightly.

'First impressions are everything, Becks. Lift your chin and play the part even if you don't think you can do it. If you don't, they'll eat you alive.'

I saw no need to add 'running from cannibalistic hunters' to my already too long list of tasks, so I did as he said, and rather than look down like I so badly wanted to, I made a point of staring back at the crowd.

A few seconds passed, and the crowd neither cheered nor booed, so I figured at least I wasn't messing up too bad.

Turning back around and coming to stand before me, Otto said, "Rebecca, you have done very well in your gauntlet, and as such, we'd like to give you this token of our appreciation."

Marco walked up to Otto and me then, carrying a long rectangular box in his arms, and as he came to a stop beside the chief, he nodded respectfully at me.

Otto opened the box, and as I looked at the blade resting inside, I could feel its power from where I stood.

"This is the Void blade," the chief said, his voice still amplified for everyone to hear. "May it serve you better than the one that wielded it before you."

'The fuck does that mean?' I wondered as I took in the sight of the weapon before me.

It was longer than the dagger Adam had given me, but it wasn't as long as what I would assume a sword would be; somewhere in between, I guessed.

The blade itself had a ridge of words running down the length of its center, and though I couldn't understand the writing, the calligraphy still glowed a pale blue when I looked at it, something within it, calling directly to something inside me.

The hilt was absolutely gorgeous. It was wrapped in light brown leather with silver adornments, and light blue gemstones were encrusted at the bottom. For a solid few seconds, I couldn't seem to take my eyes off the weapon, but soon enough, reality sunk in like a punch to the gut, and I looked back up to Otto, hoping I hadn't drooled or something equally as embarrassing while I'd been staring at the weapon.

Loud murmurs were going on through the crowd, but I ignored them as best I could as I suddenly felt a tremendous amount of anxiety coming off of Brax. I couldn't place what he was so worried about, but I couldn't exactly ask him in front of all these people either, so I had to keep going along with what was happening and remember to ask him about it later.

"Take it, and may the two sides of you always work in unison and be in perfect balance," Otto said with a barely perceptible nod at me, a solid indicator that he wanted me to pick up the blade.

Reaching out, I felt my hands tremble slightly as they got closer to the weapon, but I picked up the blade anyway and held it before me, not really knowing what my next step should be.

The Void blade felt so good in my hand, like it was always meant to be there, and instantly a little voice in the back of my head told me to take it easy, that the blade itself could be dangerous, and though I didn't know why I had that inkling, I didn't ignore it either.

Listening to that instinctual part of me, I hung it on my left hip from my utility belt, quickly clasping it into place, noticing it fit there as if it had been made to hang from my side.

It was incredibly weird to have so many weapons on me at once... well, at all, really, but I had kind of assumed that if all these powerful people thought I needed them, then I probably shouldn't argue with or resist their graciousness.

"Thank you," I said softly, but with Marco amplifying my voice, it came out sounding way louder and surer than I felt on the inside.

"You are most welcome, Rebecca," Otto said as Marco placed the empty box on a table at the edge of the stage and came back holding a large silver goblet.

"You passed your gauntlet, but you are not a true hunter until you have drunk from the hunter's goblet," he said as he reached up to take the goblet from Marco and held it in the space between us.

From where he was holding it, I could see the thick viscosity of the dark liquid inside, swirling from the small jostling of it changing hands.

"This is the hunter's elixir, and it consists of a single drop of blood from each species that lives in the five realms. It will unlock the rest of your powers, but by drinking it, you are pledging your life to maintain the balance between good and evil with the hunters."

I tried not to think about how he wanted me to drink actual blood, but it was easy because my mind was predominantly occupied with thinking about the commitment I was making.

For a solid moment, I had to wonder if this was really the life I wanted, whether I desired any other sort of outcome, and call me crazy, but it'd never even occurred to me to turn this position down until now.

I'd kind of just agreed with Brax when he showed up in my apartment, and I'd trusted in him and his knowledge of what I needed to do. I'd hardly asked myself at the end of the day if being a hunter was something I actually wanted.

But as I stood there, considering the miserable life I'd had before I'd met Brax, I knew beyond a shadow of a doubt that this was precisely what I wanted.

I couldn't have cared less about having to drink the blood then, and as I reached out and took the goblet from the chief's outstretched hands, turning it up as I brought it to my lips, I knew I was making the right choice for me.

Not because someone told me to, not because Brax thought that's what I was destined to do, and certainly not because there was an arena full of people expecting me to, but because I genuinely and honestly wanted the life this goblet, this organization could give me.

As I swallowed gulp after gulp of the coppery liquid, Otto repeated the motto that had been on the doors to the scale room, back inside headquarters.

"With the blessing of life comes the curse of purpose. With angelic and demonic blood flowing through your veins, you, the hunter, are charged with ensuring balance throughout the five realms, as well as within yourself. For no one can seek to amend the balance of others without first being balanced themselves.

Opposite and equal trials of excellence and failure, calmness and turmoil, silence and noise are key to fulfilling your purpose. Through pleasure and pain, love and hate, good and evil, a path is forged through your soul. One which you owe your life's very existence to seek out, follow, protect, and maintain. For it is this path, the one made by your soul and shaped by your past that will ensure your future, and a future for all."

By the time he was done speaking the words that were as old as the hunters themselves, I was done with the drink. However, as I pulled the goblet away from my mouth, something started happening inside me, something I knew was just terribly wrong.

'Finally,' my power said with a self-satisfied and slightly maniacal laugh from my mouth, as if they were my words instead of hers.

Immediately, dread filled every cell in my body as she fought her way to the surface, pushing me to the back of my mind and out of her way in the process, and never in my life had I been more terrified than I was right then.

CHAPTER 21

ABSINTHE

I'd seen this version of the future so many times I could've almost accurately counted the seconds it took for Becks to collapse after drinking the hunter's elixir. Without hesitation, I stepped forward quickly and caught her beneath her arms before she could fall and hit her head on the stage.

Everyone was probably still processing the fact that she'd dropped the goblet, so I knew it would take a few seconds for their brains to catch on to what had happened.

As realization crossed the chief's features and Brax started flying over to Becks and me, concern written all over his face, I said calmly, "No one needs to panic, okay? Her power is just trying to consume her, alright?"

"What?!" Brax screamed at me at the top of his lungs as his eyes got too big for his face. "How do I not panic knowing that?"

"She just needs to pick her kings and bind with them, and she'll be perfectly fine," I said as Derrick, Adam, and Tyler made their way over.

With more care than was probably necessary, I slowly took all of Becks' weapons away from her body and handed them off to whoever was there to grab them. Then, jerking my head at all of them so they'd give me some room, I laid her down gently on the stage and slid the braids out of her face.

"How is she supposed to pick her kings if she's unconscious, Absinthe," the chief asked me, and I smiled as I looked up at him.

"It's simple, really. All you need to do is ask her."

The chief looked like he couldn't understand, and a sigh escaped me despite myself.

'So, we're in that version of the future,' I thought. 'One where we're so far removed from the time of the kings and queens that those alive today have no idea how to be the conduit Becks needs to bind with her kings.'

"But how can she answer?" the chief asked almost helplessly, and I nodded as I looked down into Becks' face.

I knew I would have to facilitate her binding ceremony then, that I would have to use my power to act as the conduit between Becks and whoever she chose to be her kings. It was going to take a lot out of me to do so, but I would've done anything to see this come to fruition. I'd been waiting an eternity so far, it seemed, and finally, there was no need to wait any longer.

The crowd was losing their minds trying to see what was going on, but I paid them no mind as I said the words I knew Becks needed me to ask, words I hadn't heard in so long but still remembered as if they were etched on my soul.

"Rebecca, you must now choose who you want to help you carry this burden of power and purpose. Who is your first king?"

The purple/blue color of her natural-born power started to glow through Becks' skin, creating a halo effect around her entire body.

Simultaneously, that same color glow started to erupt from Tyler, where he stood next to us, and I fought against the smile that wanted to spread on my face at him being chosen first.

In all the versions of the future I'd seen where she'd chosen him first, he used it as proof that he was her favorite, and I could hear all of their laughter now from those visions even though none of it had transpired yet.

"What the?" he asked before the binding magic took hold of him, and his tongue grew silent as his body went rigidly still.

Quickly, I stood to face him and made sure I had all of his attention as I asked, "Tyler, do you swear to stay by Rebecca's side and help her carry this burden? Do you have what it takes to be her king?"

As soon as I asked the question, I felt my nose begin to bleed again. It was a tangible sign that this would be my last set of actions in this world. It was going to take all the life I had left in me to bind Becks to her kings, and even as I realized this was it, I couldn't find it anywhere in myself to fight it.

I wanted her to live, and to live happily with those she loved, so it didn't matter if I wasn't going to be there to see it.

Tyler spoke easily, saying, "Yes. I swear it, and I do."

Instantly, Becks' power became so bright I couldn't see her or Tyler at all in the radiant light as her power mixed with his, but as soon as the bond was in place, it began to slowly subside.

This had always been my favorite part of binding ceremonies in the past: the look.

I stared down at Becks beside me and saw her eyes open, her gaze falling on Tyler's, and his falling on hers in return, as their souls coalesced as one, and they saw each other clearly for the first time.

The moment was magical in every sense of the word, and I don't think anyone in attendance missed the love and commitment that passed between them in that moment.

A short few seconds later, the power they now shared disappeared from view entirely, and I knew it was time for me to get to work again.

Becks was still lying on the ground, unable to move as she fought her power back internally, but with the added boost from Tyler's magic, she was able to at least stay conscious.

However, the power inside her was remarkably strong, and one king would have never been enough to balance her out. She needed more.

Sinking back to my knees beside Becks' face, I looked into her eyes again as I asked, "Who is your second king?"

Immediately, she started to glow again, and this time, it was Adam who glowed with her.

The expression on his face was so full of relief that I found myself chuckling as I stood up to ask him for his acceptance of the role she was offering him.

"Adam, do you swear to stay by Rebecca's side and help her carry this burden? Do you have what it takes to be her king?"

His smile was infectious as he said, "Yes, I will, and yes, I am," and again, the brightness of their bond solidifying had me squinting.

The look they shared afterward was one of deep, heartfelt passion, and though I didn't want to intrude on their moment, the pale color of Becks' otherwise tanned skin had me worrying some.

I hadn't seen that in my previous visions, and it was not the time to stop and check out what the future held right then, but I couldn't deny the fear that crept through me when I saw it. Each new king that bound themselves to her should have made her stronger, but for some reason, the addition of Adam's power didn't seem like it offered her as much help as it should have. For that matter, neither had Tyler's.

Choosing to ignore that small hiccup right then, I squatted back down and hastily asked Becks, "Who is your third king?"

When Derrick started to glow, I became hopeful, and even through his acceptance, I thought things were going well because Becks was actually able to stand up afterward.

However, as I watched her, I could see that she was still having a hard time holding back her power from consuming her, and a dose of trepidation shot through me.

"How do you feel?" I asked her as I felt another trickle of blood flowing down my neck from my ear.

Being the conduit for her magic to bind with her new kings had torn me down even more than I'd thought it could, especially after Becks had basically shot me full force in the chest, not an hour before. It'd been everything I could do to just stand there while she was becoming a true hunter, but I'd ignored the new and agonizing pain I felt because I knew I only had to last a little while longer.

"I love all of them, Absinthe, and binding with them has definitely helped, but my power is still fighting me. I don't know if I can keep her down," she pleaded with me, and I wracked my brain for another solution.

In all the visions I'd seen of this part of her future, I'd never seen this, and honestly, I was lost as to what else she needed.

"I need one more," she said, her eyes looking so deep into mine that it felt like she was seeing right into my soul.

For a moment, I had a hard time accepting what she'd just said, but I pulled myself together and readied myself to play the part I'd agreed to play, whether it killed me or not.

"Alright," I said as I thought about the others she might choose, but before I could ask her anything else, she spoke up, cutting me off.

"My fourth king is you, Absinthe."

Right away, my body began to glow along with hers, and as outstanding as it felt to be one of the ones she wanted, I knew right then why I'd never been able to see beyond this point before.

If I accepted this role, if I chose to be one of her kings, I would be giving up my immortality altogether, and quite possibly, my magic too.

It would all go to her because things work differently for jinns.

My magic wouldn't meet hers and level out like hers had with the other men she'd chosen. Instead, it would suck the immortal life right out of me.

Still, while I was considering all this, I could see Becks getting weaker by the second as her power started to get the better of her.

She really did need me.

She needed the amount of power she was going to gain by taking mine.

And as stupid as it may have been, I gave it up willingly for her, no questions asked.

"I will help you carry your burden, and I definitely know what it takes," I said, knowing I was about to die. I knew that when her magic met mine, it would kill me, that I wouldn't be able to hang around and live up to the commitment I was making, but I lied anyway because that's what Becks needed from me right then. And I was happy to give it all up for her.

PART IV
HUNTER

CHAPTER 22

BRAX

I'd sometimes imagined life to be like a very long hallway - one where a series of curtains are draped across the path I need to travel down every few feet or so, blocking what I can see or understand of the future, almost like checkpoints.

In this hallway, you can never go backward, only forward, even though you can look back and see how far you've come whenever you want. However, unless you want to stay stuck, you have to keep pushing through those curtains and keep seeking out the next path life wants you to take.

When you get to the next curtain, you may be able to peek through some, might even have a feeling about what's on the other side because maybe you can hear noises over there, or you saw someone go through them.

But the reality is, unless you push those curtains all the way back and reveal what's been hidden from you, you will never get the dose of clarity you so desperately need - clarity that defines what you know and understand of what's been going on or what you can expect in the future at the next curtain.

The opening of the curtain was always a shift in perspective. As Becks and Absinthe started to glow, their powers merging together as one, another curtain slid all the way back in my metaphorical hallway.

Ever since we were in Heaven for Becks' trials there, it had seemed like everyone's powers were going batshit crazy, and all the way up until now, I couldn't figure out why to save my life.

Derrick had always been the one with the most self-control; it was why he was considered the leader of his team, his ability to reason despite his own feelings or thoughts on a particular matter. However, since Heaven, his power had been wanting to ooze out of his palms with almost no provocation whatsoever. He almost accidentally took out the chief when the chief told him his plans to name Becks queen tonight, but he also almost killed a stray cat that startled him as he was waiting for Becks to get ready. As if the wind could blow wrong and his magic would attack.

Adam had been fighting off and losing most of the battles with the visions that had been steadily assaulting him out of nowhere. He could no longer keep me out since he was so frazzled from the onslaught, but even when I looked in his mind, I could see that he was very close to being lost to them entirely. Like I half expected him to get lost in a vision and never wake back up; that's how strong they were.

Though Tyler always had to wrangle his beast and keep him from coming out whenever he got too emotional about things, tonight had been a remarkably harder fight than I think he'd ever experienced. Ralto was just not staying down when Tyler told him to, and was fighting for complete and ultimate control over Tyler.

Even Absinthe, the immortal jinn who was supposed to be impervious to physical pain and suffering, was bleeding and acting as if he were trying to smile through whatever it was he was feeling. He shouldn't have been able to feel anything really, pain-wise, I mean, but it was evident if you were watching him as closely as I had been. Where I'd started out watching him, purely for Becks' sake so if he stepped out of line, I could do something about it, at some point, my concern had shifted from Becks and got stuck on *his* well-being - something I'd never thought I'd do for any reason.

Which, if anything, spoke to how I had been feeling off as well.

I'd never in all my lives, not even once, turned to stone without willing it to happen, not even during any of my drunken escapades had I done such a thing, but back in Heaven, that was exactly what happened. I was not too happy about it, to say the least.

I'd had to fight that urge off, as well as a slew of other impulses just so I could maintain normalcy.

None of it had made any sense until clarity finally took shape in my mind, and I understood what had been going on.

As Becks' and Absinthe's glow started to subside, I realized that just like how Becks had needed the guys' power to help her control her own, the guys had needed hers just as much.

The closer she got to becoming a true hunter and getting the rest of her powers, the worse it got for them. For all of them. It was as if their power was peaking right as hers was, and they all needed each other to even themselves out.

My first clue had been when the panicky and pissed off feelings Tyler was feeling went away entirely as he bonded with Becks. I could hear his thoughts when that happened and had been insanely surprised when I heard him become alpha in his own mind, permanently putting Ralto in his place within him.

However, I thought that was Becks' power telling Ralto to back down.

Now that I thought about it, though, it was more likely that all of that had been Tyler's new powers he'd gotten from Becks, finally allowing him to take charge of his own body.

Another indicator was when Adam's visions completely stopped trying to blitz through his psyche once he'd bonded with Becks, as if the power she'd shared with him gave him the ability to keep them at bay.

When Derrick bonded with Becks, his magic increased exponentially; I could feel it. But it was no longer wanting to go out partying on its own whether Derrick wanted it to or not like it had been before. Even though there was tremendously more magic in him now, somehow, he had an even better hold on it than he'd ever had before, and I knew it was because of his new bond with Becks.

Absinthe was a different story, though.

I watched as the glow disappeared, and I saw the worried anticipation he was feeling written all over his face as it went away. However, when he dropped to his knees before Becks, all the air escaping his lungs, making it seem like he couldn't pull in another breath, I couldn't understand what exactly was happening.

Absinthe's chest of armor began to disappear right before our eyes, leaving him topless on the stage as shimmery red smoke started to trickle out of his body and wrap loosely around him. Specks of gold started seeping out of him slowly, dissipating in the air like ashes from a fire, and the cuffs on his wrists fell away to clank across the floor before they disappeared altogether as well.

Becks dropped down before the jinn and took his hands in hers, a look of torment spreading across her face. I couldn't hear what she was thinking, but I could tell by her expression that she was not handling what was happening in front of her very well.

Absinthe's purple eyes stayed locked on Becks the entire time, but when the smoke dispersed, his eyes seemed to close of their own accord, and his head dropped to his chest as his body went completely limp except for where he still sat on his knees.

"Absinthe," Becks called as she shook his hands in hers, probably trying to wake him up or something.

At first, he didn't respond, and a new and altogether unsettling fear for how Becks would feel if she lost him spread through me. I may not have liked the jinn, but I didn't actually want him to die, not when I knew how Becks felt about him, anyway.

However, as his head slowly began to lift, and his eyes finally met back up with Becks', a small smile played on his lips as he stared at her, and relief splashed through me.

"I'm still here," he said softly, in a tone full of satisfied relief.

"Did you think you wouldn't be?" Becks immediately questioned him, an undeniable sliver of anger sliding into her voice.

Absinthe smiled even more as he considered her, then sent a hand out to cup her cheek. "It might've crossed my mind a time or two, but I've never been so happy to be wrong in all my life."

"What the hell? You thought this would kill you, and you accepted anyway? What's wrong with you?" Becks said as her temper got the better of her, and she slapped Absinthe's shoulder one good time for good measure.

Absinthe's joyful and playful laugh sounded through the arena right then, though I could still hear that it sounded like he'd been through something significant.

"I guess you are what's wrong with me?" he said with a questioning tone and a smile that Becks returned when he finished his thought. "But I'd take you on and give it all up in a heartbeat over and over again if it meant I got to hear you say you wanted me as your king too."

Suddenly, the crowd surrounding us burst into cheers, and since I'd nearly forgotten all about them, the surprise of it made me jump into the air on my wings and spin as I took them all in.

They'd witnessed the whole thing, and as I realized that fact, I noted they all seemed to be happy about what was going on too, and some part of me was relieved by it.

"Rebecca," the chief said, pulling her attention to him and quieting the crowd with one word. "Please stand."

Becks stood and walked over to him as my eyes got big and watery again, knowing what was about to happen.

When she stood in front of the chief, I could feel the nervousness she was feeling slipping through our connection, and I sent what little reassurance I could toward her in hopes that it would help.

"Brax," Chief called, pulling me out of my thoughts about Becks, and I flew over to him as he gestured for me to float next to Becks, facing a section of the crowd.

"Derrick, Adam, Tyler, Absinthe," he then called. "Please come stand here."

All the guys lined up a step behind and to the side of Becks and me before Chief walked forward to address the crowd.

"Hunters," he started, his voice booming through the arena and sending a chill down my spine.

"I present to you, Queen Becks..." the chief called as he looked back at Becks and motioned for her to take a step forward.

As the crowd whooped and shrieked, I heard Becks' thoughts echo through my mind.

'He called me Becks,' and the smiles on both of our faces at the thought were filled with an almost overwhelming amount of emotion I couldn't quite describe.

Moving right along, none the wiser to what Becks had just been thinking, the chief motioned for me to fly a little farther forward as he said, "The royal familiar, Brax..."

'Royal?' I thought with surprise before Becks' thoughts broke into my mind.

'You can bet your pixie titty loving ass you're royal. If I'm in this, you're coming with me.' The look on her face was full of blushing happiness and playful sincerity, and I couldn't deny how happy I was too in that moment.

She was still panicking hard on the inside, barely keeping it together with everything that was going on, but that was one of the most incredible things about Becks: despite the turmoil she might be feeling, she could compartmentalize, still had a sense of humor, and could put on a mask if she needed to.

"Kings..." the chief's voice called out, "Tyler, Adam, Derrick, and Absinthe."

The crowd lost their ever-loving minds as we were all presented to them, and as the chief turned around to face us, he started clapping as well, his eyes filling with unshed tears, the pride in his expression unquestionable.

We all stood there and accepted what was going on, but a quick search through everyone's minds told me that we were all feeling the same things. Overwhelm, an unreasonable amount of pressure from the level of responsibility we now had, pride, worry... the list could go on.

After he got his emotions under control again, the chief turned back to the crowd, quieting them as he said, "I know that this comes as a shock to most of you, and it comes to us in the same way, but there is no denying what's happened here today, no doubt of who these young people were meant to become.

These are your new monarchs, and though this transition will have its difficulties, I know this is the team that we all need leading us.

I will be here, and so will Chief Sato of Binaria East to help with the restructuring of our proud organization, and though we won't be your leaders anymore, I know we will be leaving you in good hands.

I'm sure you are all just dying to hear from her, so I'll quit jabbering and let her up here. Without further ado, Queen Becks," the chief said.

I could feel the mind-blowing alarm, dismay, and distress running through Becks as he motioned for her to step forward and address the hunters, but her steps never faltered, and her voice never hesitated as she put up the front she needed to portray right then.

The only outward indication of the turmoil she was feeling on the inside was the small clearing of her throat before she began speaking, and I couldn't have been prouder of her as her words flowed through the arena.

"Hunters," she said, and you could hear a pin drop with how intently everyone was hanging on every word she said.

"Have you ever run with fairies?

Or stared at a flower with a pixie?

Befriended a human?

Walked past a demon and wondered what his story was?"

She started walking as she talked, getting more comfortable with what she was doing with every second that passed.

"Have you ever swum with Merfolk?

Or been sucked into an incubus' atmosphere?"

I had no idea where she was going with her questioning, but I had to trust that her instincts were on point, so I just went along with it.

"It's magical, right? This life that we have?"

She paused for a second, and I could see that the hunters' eyes staring down at Becks were shining with nostalgia and a sense of wonder. As if within a few questions, Becks had gotten them to tap back into what drove them as hunters in the first place.

"I may not have grown up in this organization like you all did, and I may be new to your ways, but I am not new to the magic that lives in this world or the purity and perfectness of it, no matter which form it takes.

In fact, I've dreamt about the creatures of this world my entire life, my only desires being to see them, interact with them, protect them… to live in a world where they exist.

And I think that's what all of you want as well, to live in a world where the balance is maintained and where every living creature, magical or not, has a fighting chance."

Pride swelled inside me at her words, and as subtly as possible, I wiped a tear from my eye that wanted to escape.

"I know this organization has had its issues, that you've seen bad things, experienced terrible heartache for the sake of doing your jobs, and I am not promising to right every wrong that has ever taken place, but I am vowing that I will do my damndest to make things better in the future."

Her cheeks went pink for a second as she looked back at me and thought-asked, *'Oh, shit! Can I cuss?'*

Immediately a laugh burst through my mouth that I couldn't prevent, and I said, "It's okay; I'm sure they don't mind you cussing." Marco was still amplifying our voices, and as the people heard that, a laugh resounded around the stadium, and a few cheers went up, further proving my point.

"Well, good," Becks said as she glanced down at her feet for a second. "'Cause I've got a mouth on me," she laughed, which only had the crowd laughing more, right along with her.

"Anyway," she started back up again. "I don't want to take up all of your time, but there is one important thing about me that I want you all to know."

She paused again at the perfect point as if she'd been taking public speaking classes her whole life, but I knew for sure she hadn't.

Looking back up at the crowd, a solid set to her chin and shoulders, she said, "I have always questioned power and everyone who wields it because I know the damage it can cause when it's not kept in check.

This is another vow I will make to you now: I will always question my power as if I were you, and I urge you to do the same. To question everything and everyone, no matter their position, because it's that constant questioning and accountability that will ensure change where it's needed and reassurance where it's doubted.

I didn't ask to be queen, but I will accept my place graciously and do everything I can to be the best I can be at it because you deserve it... because the creatures we all love so much deserve it... because this world needs it. And if that means stepping up as your queen, so be it. I will do what is right by you and by the creatures of this world, no matter what it costs me, I promise."

The crowd erupted into joyful cheers as she stepped back beside me, and Chief stepped back into her place. Immediately, each of the guys placed a hand on her somewhere, offering Becks the reassurance they knew she needed. Still, as Chief thanked everyone, gave out instructions on next steps, and dismissed them, I couldn't take my eyes off of Becks, nor she of me as our silent conversation took shape in our minds and quiet tears flowed down each of our cheeks.

I was so proud of her, so happy that she'd finally made it to this point - a point even I'd never dreamed she'd reach given her history, and as our hands reached out to one another, hope started to seep into me, true and strong, for the first time in a really long while.

CHAPTER 23

BECKS

"Way to put me on the spot back there, Chief," I said as we all came back into existence after teleporting into Otto's office. "Like really, what the actual fuck?"

Honestly, I'd barely been keeping my wits about me from the time Absinthe sent me to the gauntlet in the first place, not to mention the fact that I'd already had a freaking panic attack today, but by this point, I was about to lose my fucking mind.

Yes, I'd had the break of the intermission to help recenter me some, and I'd thoroughly enjoyed all the time I'd had to spend with the guys, but in no way had it offered me the mental space I needed to wrap my mind around everything that was going on and everything that was being asked... no, demanded of me.

Yes, I'd made it through the gauntlet, but I had more questions now that I'd gone through than I'd had before I went, and that was saying something.

And as if all that hadn't been bad enough, there was everything that had happened at that mindfuck of a ceremony I'd just been through.

I felt like my life was spinning out of control, like I was lost in a whirlwind of new responsibilities without a clue as to how to handle them.

Here I was, queen of the hunters, yet I had no idea what that meant. I had all this power and no idea what I could do exactly or how I was supposed to use it. I'd won all these weapons, but I'd never once shot a bow, wielded a sword, or even thought about poisoning someone, yet here I was with all these shiny new tools at my disposal, and a destiny which basically demanded I figure that shit out ASAP.

I needed answers.

I needed space.

I needed time - time where I could put things in perspective, where nothing could be asked of me for a while, where I could hopefully get to a point where I felt like I had a handle on at least most of the things I was facing. But as my experience with the hunters had taught me so far, they weren't just handing that kind of thing out all willy nilly.

I was going to have to demand it or take it without asking, I already knew it, and I was not looking forward to that at all.

"I know it seems like I just sprang all of that on you..." Otto started, but I cut him off in my anger.

"It doesn't just *seem* like it, Otto. You absolutely sprung it on me." I thought for a second before I turned an accusatory eye on everyone in the room.

"You know what? You all did! Not one of you prepared me for this... for any of it!

It's like you all have just expected me to roll with the punches and hidden agendas, to just say 'okay' to whatever it is that's going on under the guise of 'stopping the apocalypse,' when I can look back and see countless opportunities where you could have clued me in, where you could've given me a head's up, where you could have prepared me for what I was going to have to face, so it wasn't shoved down my throat!"

I took a much-needed breath, but I was far from finished, and as I took in the looks on all the guys' faces around me, my anger spiked even higher at their pity.

"I may have wanted to end my life before I met you, Brax, but once you came into my life, I didn't think twice about doing what you said. I followed along, worked out, did what you all told me to do, and waited for answers. I waited for answers from all of you. Fuck, I'm *still* waiting for answers!

I didn't argue much, and I hardly ever complained when you guys got all tight-lipped about what was going on or what needed to happen.

And dammit, I said goodbye to my friend for this!" I screamed as Ava's face and the pain of losing her that I'd been trying to ignore since the night I left her poured out of me as tears filled my eyes.

"I went through your stupid gauntlet, and I faced my fears," I said as sobs forced themselves into my voice.

"I've taken 'my place,'" I said with sarcastic air quotes, "as queen, and accepted you guys as my kings. So, we're basically married, and I've never even been on a real fucking date with any of you!"

My voice was becoming more challenging to understand around my tears, even to my own ears, but I didn't care.

"And now I've literally got the world on my shoulders, and you, Otto, decide, 'Oh, I'll just throw her to the fucking wolves and make her speak to the crowd. I bet that'll be fun.'

Well, it was not fun, you prick! I was scared shitless, and some fucking how, now you have the audacity to be like, 'If it *seems* like I sprang it on you.'

Fuck that sugarcoated bullshit of a lie! And fuck all of you for going along with it too! I've had enough!"

Angrily, I swiped the tears from my face as the rage inside me settled into sadness at the impossibility of it all.

Without thought, I fell back onto the couch behind me, crying into my hands with my elbows on my knees. A couple of the braids that had fallen loose in my hair dropped down around my hands as I begged, "Can we please, just take a break now? I don't think I can take much more of this."

No one said anything at first, but I felt the cushions I was sitting on shift when a couple of them sat down next to me, and I could feel the presence of the rest of them close by as well.

"I'm very sorry, Becks," Otto's voice pulled me up short by the sincerity I heard in it, and I moved my hands so I could see him.

He was squatting down in front of me, and as my eyes met his, he sent a concerned hand to my shoulder. "No one should have to go through what you've had to deal with. Especially not a hunter that's destined to become what you are.

I wish I could've waited, I really do," he said before he took a deep breath. "But I didn't have much of a choice."

"What do you mean?" I asked softly, my energy spent after my mental breakdown.

"As soon as it was confirmed in your gauntlet that you were supposed to be queen, you had a target the size of the world on your back."

I hadn't thought of that before, and instantly, a shiver went down my spine.

"The Order of Division is a group of disgruntled hunters…"

"I know who they are," I cut him off again, unable to maintain societal niceties at that point, recalling a part of the conversation I'd had with Derrick during my intermission.

Otto cleared his throat some but continued on undeterred. "Well, I knew that I had to get in front of them. They were going to be doing everything they could to kill you and your kings; there was no doubt in my mind.

Suppose I didn't go ahead and proclaim you queen in front of as many hunters as possible. In that case, they could've taken that opportunity to do what they have been trained to do, and though I know they're still out there, probably planning an attack on all of you as we speak, at least now they're going to have a harder time doing it because everyone knows about you now."

Carefully, he removed his hand from my shoulder and sat back on his heels.

"Also, I don't think there's a way I could've sprung that on the hunters without having you speak to them personally. They needed to hear from you after that. You had to become real to them, and the only way I could see to make that happen was to let you speak."

He paused for a breath before he asked, "Do you think you would have agreed to such a thing had I asked you beforehand?"

I wanted to say that yes, I would have, but I knew better. I hate speaking in front of people. I would've done everything I could've thought of to get out of it had I known it was coming.

I shook my head at him as I accepted what he was saying.

"You did an excellent job, though," he said easily. "That speech couldn't have been better if you'd had weeks to prepare for it because you were your most genuine self up there, speaking from your heart and soul as you talked to them, and I can tell you now, you got through to them, I promise. They heard you."

"He's right," Brax said from beside the chief, where he sat cross-legged on the floor, his big wings hanging limply at his back. "I could feel it. The hunters may still be a little wary, but they're hopeful, and that's the most we could've asked for on such short notice."

It took me a second, but eventually, I nodded at the chief as he started to get up, leaning heavily on Absinthe's shoulder for help.

When I looked at him questioningly, he rubbed his leg and said simply, "I'm not a spring chicken anymore, Becks, and some wounds never heal all the way."

I tried not to examine that too closely as he backed up and took a seat in the chair across from me.

My breath was still showing the aftermath of my crying session, and more tears were just a wrong word away, but I was calming down some by just having the guys near me, by the fact that they all hadn't gone running for the hills when I'd lost it on them and probably looked like a complete nutjob.

"I know we haven't told you everything," Derrick said from my right, and I turned my head in his general direction, though my eyes were still plastered to the floor as my thoughts kept swirling. "We didn't tell you a lot because for a large chunk of what was going on, we didn't even know ourselves what was happening. The rest of the time, we were trying not to overwhelm you with information and the severity of the different situations. And for your intermission, we avoided talking about most anything that could possibly upset you because that's what we thought you needed from us at the time."

I sighed a heavy breath as I let his words run through my head.

It made sense, everything he said, but it still didn't make me feel any better. By hiding what I was going to have to face in the gauntlet, I went in unprepared and frightened beyond belief. By not telling me about what the chief had planned until we were about to step outside, I'd accidentally shot my power through Absinthe's chest and sent Brax flying down the hallway. And by failing to mention what I was expected to do as queen, I still felt remarkably misplaced in this world.

"I'm sorry," he said. "We all are."

My gaze shot up to his honey brown eyes. The look in them was sincere, and though I was still angry, there was no way I couldn't accept his apology when he looked at me like that, no way I couldn't forgive all of them.

"I forgive all of you," I said as I sent my eyes back to the floor. For some reason, it just felt better to stare at the carpet than it did to look at anyone right then.

"We know you've been doing your best, that you've been trying your hardest to do what's been required of you, and we should've told you what a good job you've been doing, but we didn't," Tyler said from my left, and a lump started to form in my throat at his words.

"And I know you gave up your friend for this life," he kept talking, but as soon as the words left his mouth, a new wave of sadness flooded through me and my face squinched up as tears began filling my eyes again.

Ava's face, her attitude, her friendship raced through my mind as I put my hands back over my eyes. "I miss her so much," I said, and I felt

Derrick's and Tyler's hands fall on my back in silent support, but the motions didn't help that much.

"You know," Otto said as if an idea had just occurred to him. "You are technically queen now, and the decision to tell her would be your decision to make."

Hope and worry both spread through me as I dropped my hands and looked at him.

"You mean, tell her about all this?" I questioned him like he was crazy.

His smile was soft and understanding as he said, "Well, honestly, it might even be a good idea to keep her close since she means so much to you. If the wrong person found out about her and your affection for her, they could use her against you. If you're queen, you make the rules, so you wouldn't have to listen to old geezers like me that have never had a human matter to them as much as she does to you."

The overwhelming happiness that floated through me at the idea of having Ava back in my life sent hypotheticals running through my mind instantly. Images of her staying off the drugs, getting out of the halfway house, of introducing her to the creatures of this world...

My thoughts trailed off as I asked, "But how can I tell her? Humans can't see the supernatural. She'd think I really was crazy."

Adam chuckled a little from the other side of Tyler. "I'm sure you could give her the gift of sight with all the power you have now."

My eyes got big as I leaned forward to see past Tyler and look at him. "You think I can do that? For real?"

Absinthe spoke up from the floor before Adam could answer. "Becks, I don't think there's anything your power couldn't do if you set your mind to it. Hell, for that matter, when we all combine our powers, I don't think there's a thing in the world that could stop us. Even if I have lost most of mine."

"What do you mean, you've lost your power?" I asked bewildered.

"Not all of it," he said with a smile in my direction. "I'm still a jinn, but I gave up my immortality and a lot of my power to bind with you."

I couldn't speak for a solid minute as I just stared at him, not knowing what to say to that.

"It's okay, Becks," he said when I didn't say anything right away. "I'm much happier with less now than I ever was when I had all of it."

I didn't know what else to do, so I climbed down onto the floor and wrapped my arms around him.

Words were failing me, but as he hugged me back without question, I knew my body was doing all the talking my mouth couldn't, and in his return embrace, I knew he understood what I meant.

When I finally pulled away a few minutes later, I realized through our touch that I felt a connection with him, kind of like the ones I had with all the other guys, and even though it strengthened with our physical contact, it wasn't the same as it was with the others.

Sitting back down on the couch, I turned my attention to Brax.

"Don't you think you should accept Absinthe now?" I asked my familiar, putting him on the spot. "He needs to be connected just as much as these other guys do, especially now."

Brax's sandy-colored eyes looked at me like I'd just asked him to turn a baseball into a flower, but instead of saying anything to argue with me, he stood up, squared his little shoulders, and leveled Absinthe with a glare purely his own.

"You're basically a human with powers now, jinn. If you hurt her, so help me…"

"Brax," I said, cutting off his threat. I did not have the patience for it right then.

"Fine," Brax said as he started to glow, and Absinthe went as stiff as a tree trunk.

Soon Brax was too bright to look at, and Absinthe looked like he was in pain. I could see him gritting his teeth, his fists clenching in his lap as he stared at Brax, and I knew that something was happening.

A few minutes later, Brax went back to normal, and his entire demeanor toward Absinthe changed immediately as he said, "Well, damn. I never would've expected that."

Absinthe smiled knowingly, as Brax said, "Welcome to the team," and sat back down with a smile on his face.

"What? You wouldn't have expected what?" I asked.

Brax sighed but answered me anyway. "This fucker has been

telling the truth the whole time, and he matches up perfectly with you, just like these other guys."

I smiled as I blushed, but I couldn't find it in me to care about what my face was doing.

"Well," Otto said. "This is a first. I have to admit I had my reservations, but since all that is true, yes, Absinthe. Welcome to the team."

Absinthe actually blushed then, his purple eyes dipping to the floor in front of him for a second, and all that did was make me smile at him.

"I hate to break up this healthy conversation we have going, but Becks, we really do need to talk about the state of things now," Otto said, and I sighed as I nodded.

"Alright, let's hear it," I said, crossing my arms over my chest as I leaned back on the couch.

The chief smiled good-naturedly and asked, "Well, I was kind of going to say the same thing to you, Becks."

Though my mind immediately got the humor and chuckled a little at his words, comprehension took another second before it solidified in my brain, then all traces of humor vanished completely.

"You want me to say what we need to do? Already? No direction of any kind? Just... spit out orders or whatever?" I asked, quickly heading right back into that overwhelming feeling I'd all but gotten past.

"No, not necessarily," Otto said, still smiling. "I was thinking we should all hear your ideas, hear what you think. You have a unique perspective, having come into this organization the way you did, and I don't doubt that you've picked up on some things that need to change. Am I right?"

It didn't take me long to consider his words before I nodded my head hesitantly at him.

"Alright, well, what are some things that you know need to be fixed right away?"

"First and foremost, would be Philippa," I said with hardly a thought.

Her plight had been so heavy on my shoulders that it had been nearly impossible to carry, and if there was any way that we could change her situation for the better, I wanted to do it.

"Give me five minutes," Otto said before he disappeared from his spot, leaving all of us looking after him, wondering what he was up to.

~

A SHORT TIME LATER, but what was much longer than five minutes, Otto showed back up with Philippa in tow. She was clinging tightly to a bag of blood as her sleepy eyes roamed over all of us.

She dropped the blood bag immediately and rushed over to Brax, where she jumped on top of him in a big baby hug that had us all laughing at her cuteness.

However, once she heard my laugh, Philippa turned and did the same thing she'd done to Brax, to me.

She hugged me tightly, and I don't know what told me to do it or why, but I stood up with her and walked away from everyone to where there was a clear spot away from any furniture. I set her down easily and sat on my knees in front of her, holding her tiny hands in mine.

I was acting on instinct alone, and honestly, I had no idea what I was doing, but I didn't question it as my eyes closed, and I knew I was beginning to glow.

Words spilled from my mouth that I had no real control over, but as I spoke them, I knew I was doing the right thing.

"You've been trapped and imprisoned for long enough, child of the night. Now is the time to face the pain and the daylight your body originally rejected. Now is the time to grow again. Now is the time to become who you were meant to be."

I felt my power growing and working, pulling from my kings in the process, but after a few seconds, I knew whatever I'd done had taken effect.

It was a weird feeling. All my thoughts and concerns about Philippa coalesced into whatever spell I'd cast, and only once it was over did I ever think to question it.

As I opened my eyes, Philippa was still standing there holding my hands, but the awareness behind those big blue eyes of hers was unmistakable.

"Did you just give her the ability to grow?" Otto asked as he stood up and came over to Philippa and me, the tone of his voice sounding both happy and perplexed.

"Yes," I said, knowing I was telling the truth, though I had no idea how I knew to do such a thing. "And though she is still a vampire, her original diseases are gone forever."

"I thought the vampirism had done that already?" Brax asked. "I mean, as a vampire, she was already able to go out in the sunlight and sleep."

I nodded and explained, despite not knowing what I would say before it came out of my mouth. "Yes, she was able to do those things, but she still couldn't feel physical pain, which is remarkably scary. She couldn't be in the sunlight for too long. She was also unable to grow.

Now she can feel pain and protect herself from it. She can go in the sunlight, and every person she turns will be able to as well. But most importantly, she will continue to grow like a normal child until her body reaches maturity."

I stood up, shaking my head to offset the spell I seemed to be under, and looked around at the men surrounding me while Philippa hugged my leg.

"Um..." I said, the obvious question I was trying to ask, sitting heavy in the space between us.

"I guess you don't need answers after all," Absinthe joked, but I could find no humor in what he'd said.

"What do you mean?"

Walking over to me, he threw one arm around my shoulder as he said, "Your power has mixed with all of ours, except for the chief, obviously. Meaning it mixed with mine. I'm guessing you just started saying those things, casting that spell without thought, am I right?"

I nodded at him as his smile grew.

"Your power and instincts know what's really going on whether your conscious mind does too or not. It's how I knew what was going on even though I was trapped in a cave in Alaska. Somehow you've taken that and made it even better!"

I couldn't even begin to try and understand that just yet, so I lifted Philippa up into my arms and hugged her since that's what felt like the best thing to do right then.

No matter where the power to do what I'd just done came from, or how surprising it had been, I was elated about what I'd been able to do for her, and beyond hopeful for the quality of life she was going to have now that I'd done it.

"Well, that solves that issue," Otto chuckled. "On to the next?"

CHAPTER 24

BECKS

"*D*oes everything need to be figured out right now?" I asked, thoroughly feeling the exhaustion from the last few days settling deep inside my bones.

Otto sighed but said, "I guess not." Then seeming to rethink his stance, he added, "If you could open the portals the Mer king closed, that would be a great help, though. I think everything else can wait. He died before he was able to reverse the spell he'd used, and Mer families are still being kept apart because they're still closed."

"Do you have any idea how I should go about fixing that?" I asked him, but it was Derrick that spoke up.

"If it's anything like opening a regular portal, I may be able to help. I mean, I can show you how I normally do it, and then we can trial and error it until we figure it out, I guess."

"That sounds like the best plan I've heard," Otto said, relief visible in his stance as well as his tone. "If you do that, I'll see what I can get started with here on the reorganization stuff. There will be a lot of work needed to change everything over to how things will run with monarchs again, but you're right. You guys all need a break after everything you've been through.

Why don't you take a week while you're trying to figure out the portal situation, and by the time you get back, I should have a good head start on everything here."

I was blown away by what he was offering. An entire week where all we had to do was figure out how to close some portals? I mean, I didn't have the faintest clue about how I would do that exactly, but after what had just happened with Philippa, I wasn't feeling too bad about my chances.

"Chief, that sounds amazing," Tyler said as he leaned his head back, closed his eyes, and sighed. "A week off?" He brought his head back up and looked at Otto. "I could kiss you right now, old man."

We all laughed at that, and soon after, we were saying goodbye to Philippa and the chief. The plan was that she would stay with him since he had access to the blood she'd need, and that we could come back any time we wanted to see her.

He promised me that no decision would be made without my consent when it came to her ability to heal the infected vampires, and I promised him in return that I would try and come up with a solution as soon as possible.

Once they both walked out of the office, leaving me with my familiar and the rest of my team, I looked back at Tyler. I reached out to put my hand on his shoulder so we could teleport, but before my hand or anyone else's for that matter could touch him, we were already standing in the living room of the beach safe house.

"How the fuck?" Tyler asked, his eyes wide, his eyebrows nearly reaching the top of his head.

"What? You thought your power had stayed the same after binding with Becks?" Absinthe asked Tyler with a chuckle. "You thought she was the only one who's power increased?"

Tyler didn't say anything, the shock of the fact that he'd just teleported all of us with his mind alone, stopping even his usual snarky comments.

Smiling, I said, "I'm still gonna touch you when you teleport me 'cause I want to."

That snapped him out of his shock and into a new one. I could see the heat in his eyes to prove it, and I fully intended to keep my word as I saw it.

"You better," he said, and my girly parts jumped involuntarily, the demand in his tone catching me off guard but enticing me in a way I'd never felt before.

Brax yawned big and loud then, pulling all of our attention to him where he'd plopped himself down on the bar. "I don't know about you guys, but I'm beat. How about we call it a night, huh?"

Instantly, I was yawning too, and all I wanted was to sleep for an ungodly amount of time. "Sounds good to me," I said on the ass end of a yawn.

"Absinthe, there's an extra bedroom at the end of the hall you can have," Derrick said as he pointed in the direction he was talking about.

Walking over to me, he gave me a big hug, kissed the top of my head, and whispered in my ear, "I am so proud of you, Becks. I hope you know that." Then, seeming to get an idea, he added, "If you want some company tonight, don't hesitate to come to me. You know where I'll be."

Derrick pulled away from me and smiled as he turned on his heel and made for his bedroom, sending one hand in the air as he said, "I'll see you all in the morning. Goodnight."

Next was Adam. He came over and hugged me in much the same way as Derrick had, even adding, "Feel free to come snuggle with me if you want," before he too walked down the hallway.

Tyler was, of course, the showoff, though. When he came over to me, he lightly grabbed my chin, tilted my head back, and kissed me without an ounce of warning. Not that I needed a warning since I'd wanted him to do it anyway.

He said I could come to his bed too, and before he released me from his hug, he slapped my ass with one hand while he smiled down dangerously at me. I didn't know whether to be mad or flattered at first, but as he turned to leave and more heat rose inside me, I knew I didn't mind his actions all that much. In fact, that slap had felt damn good, if I was honest with myself.

Brax just giggled at me and flew off to my bedroom to no doubt make himself comfortable in my bed as always, and though I rolled my eyes at him, I smiled at his back too.

When Absinthe was the last one standing there, he surprised me because he didn't move toward me like the others had.

With barely a thought, I found myself walking over to him instead, something inside my gut telling me that's what he wanted me to do. As I got right in front of him, his hands reached out to each one of my hips to grip me lightly, and it didn't occur to me to mind as I sent my hands to his still bare chest.

"What are you thinking about?" he asked me softly, his voice doing something to my brain with the sensual tone of it.

Feeling slightly embarrassed, I said honestly, "About our kiss."

His smile faltered some as his face turned somewhat serious.

"We can repeat it if you sleep in my new room with me."

"But only then?" I couldn't help but smile as I asked him.

A sinful smirk played on his lips as he let go of me and started walking backwards to his room, a challenging expression on his face as he disappeared behind the door a few seconds later.

'Ugh, these guys,' I thought as my whole body ached with a need I wasn't familiar with. 'What the hell do I do now? Do I actually choose between them? Maybe I should just sleep next to Brax again.'

I quickly dismissed that idea, though, because as much as I loved Brax, that was the last option I wanted to choose.

Making up my mind, I walked to my door and peeked in, eyeing Brax in the center of my bed again, just where I thought he'd be.

"Hey," I said, getting his attention. "I'm not sleeping in here tonight. I hope that's okay."

Brax didn't even sit up or open his eyes as he responded. "I know, and it's about damn time too. Why do you think I always lay here like this? You don't belong in this bed." I could see his playful smile from where I was standing.

Some part of me wanted to balk at what he'd said, but I didn't know why, and I couldn't actually bring myself to say anything anyway because a feeling of happiness too strong to ignore slid through me right then.

"Goodnight, Brax," I ended up saying around a smile before I closed the door to my room and headed to Adam's.

He'd told me about his nightmares during my intermission, and since then, I'd been hoping I'd be able to offer him some form of comfort from them, even if it was only with my presence.

I turned the knob on his door silently, but he shot up in the bed as if I'd busted in to hold him at gunpoint.

However, after he realized it was me, his face softened, and he smiled genuinely.

"There is no way I thought you'd come to me tonight," he said, the blush in his cheeks apparent, even as he pulled the covers back and slid over to make room for me.

Still, I had a moment of hesitation, and I asked, "Have you changed your mind?"

"Fuck no," he answered quickly as if that had never been a possibility, and the fervor I heard in his voice, despite the words that didn't sound natural coming from him, just had me thinking he really meant what he said. "Get over here."

Shutting the door behind me, the room was plunged into darkness except for what moonlight crept through the blinds, and I made my way over to his bed easily enough.

I stood there for a second, debating whether I should just sleep in what I was wearing, but ultimately, I decided against it.

I undressed down to only my t-shirt and underwear before I climbed in beside him, laying down with my back up against his bare chest.

His left arm was already in place to act as my pillow, and as I snuggled into him and the blankets, his right arm wrapped around my ribs, squeezing me to him tightly.

I was reveling in the feeling of being in his arms like that, but I was also a big ol' ball of nerves as well.

We were basically married, and along that same path of thought, this was technically our wedding night.

I may have grown up in an insane asylum, but even I knew that meant sex, and lots of it if I wasn't mistaken. At least, I thought that was how it worked for the humans. I had no idea if hunters were the same way.

When I thought about it, though, I realized that was exactly what I wanted, exactly what my body needed.

It was a newfound feeling for me, and a fierce one at that if the heat spreading through me was any kind of indication. Actually desiring intimacy and physical contact was way outside the norm from where my thoughts usually traveled, but as I laid there, it was almost all I could think about.

A few seconds later, I felt Adam lift up some and bring his nose to the back of my neck, and at the feel of him there, a little gasp pulled through my throat.

He breathed me in deeply, resting his forehead against the back of my head, and I didn't know how to not let that action go straight to my heart, nor why I would want to stop it in the first place.

There was just something so... intense about it, about the way my body responded to his when he did it again a few seconds later.

I didn't think about moving before I sent my right hand back behind me. My fingertips ran through the hair on the side of his head behind his ear as I turned slightly to face him, anticipation and an insane amount of uncertainty filling every part of me.

It was like I knew he'd agreed to be my 'king' or whatever, that he'd told me he loved me, and I'd told him I loved him too, but there was still that little self-deprecating bitch in the back of my mind spewing thoughts of potential rejection at me as if none of that had been real.

His lips found mine in the dark without issue, though, and the hand he'd had around my ribs came up to rub my cheek lightly, reassuring me in a way I desired desperately.

I didn't know what I was supposed to do, but it seemed like my body did without question, so I did what felt right as sparks flew around in my belly, my mind finally shutting off in the best way possible.

As his tongue started to dance with mine, I was nearly overcome by want and need, and as the passion between us kicked up in both speed and intensity, my feelings for him only grew stronger.

He pulled away for only a split second as he gently rolled me to my back beside him, effectively trapping my right arm underneath him in the crux of his shoulder joint, offering my right hand unfettered access to the smoothness of his back while the rest of me lay before him.

Adam cupped my cheek again as he brought his lips down to mine, but after a few seconds, that hand started sliding down the side of my neck.

Alarm bells were going off in my brain, but rational thought was cut off from reaching me by that point. They could have just as easily been excitement bells if I thought about it, but I didn't. I let Adam continue his slow trail down my side and reveled in every second he spent doing so.

As his fingers traveled from my left hip, sliding across the lowest parts of my belly, a sound escaped me at the surprise of how good that motion felt, and upon hearing it, I thought it only spurred Adam on even more.

His fingers dipped into the front of my underwear gradually, finding my clit a moment later as another moan escaped me, but this time, there was a moan of his own joining up with mine.

Hearing that sound from him was almost my undoing; I loved it so much, and as his fingers slipped between my folds and dove slowly inside me in time with the rhythmic beating of my heart, I felt my whole body begin to tremble in his hands.

There was something so erotic and sensual about the way he made me come twice while I still had my underwear on, but after a little while, the presence of my underwear became more of a hindrance than a turn on, and with barely a second thought, they disappeared from my body, right along with my t-shirt and bra.

A shocked gasp tore from both of us as we realized what I'd done, but in short order, it was followed by small giggles as Adam dropped his head to my chest, his hand still working me into a frenzy.

He didn't stay there long before his mouth was capturing one of my nipples. As his teeth gripped it lightly, his tongue sliding across it a few times in sync with the pace of his skilled fingers, again, I was like putty in his hands as my right hand grabbed onto his back, my fingernails digging into his flesh.

Suddenly, I found my other hand reaching for him, pulling him closer to me.

I just couldn't seem to get close enough to him to satisfy whatever I was feeling, and as the thought, 'I need him inside me,' flew frantically through my mind, I realized exactly what I wanted in that moment.

Adam didn't fight me, and no words passed between us as he succumbed to my desires without hesitation.

His fingers left me as he pulled away, and I tried not to pout since I was confident he wouldn't leave me wanting.

He freed his erection and slid out of his boxers before he moved right up in between my aching thighs, stopping just short of everything I wanted right then.

The feel of him there between my legs, right outside my entrance, had me nearly squirming to have him inside me. As he held himself above me and sent his hand to the side of my face again, my anxiousness was doused with an overwhelming amount of mushy feelings I just couldn't quite describe.

And when he kissed me again, slowly and deliberately controlling the pace as he finally entered me, sheathing himself all the way inside me, I became his entirely in that moment, another moan escaping both of us at the rightness of the feeling.

Adam dropped his forehead to mine, and I felt the shuddering breath he took before he whispered, "You're so perfect, Becks."

I nearly came again right then and there.

But as he started moving, his pace quickening, I couldn't hold out any longer if I'd tried. I came around him, completely enamored by every aspect of him and what he was doing, lost to Adam entirely.

His release followed soon after that, and once he collapsed to the bed beside me, both of us spent and satisfied, I knew it was safe for me to cuddle up to him, to lay my head on his chest and curl my leg around his.

I didn't doubt whether he'd let me for even a second, that self-deprecating voice in my head knowing full well there was nothing to second guess here. There was some kind of unspoken power in that knowledge, some sort of unbreakable reassurance that solidified inside me at that moment, and as I drifted off to sleep, I felt more safe and content than I thought I ever had in my life.

CHAPTER 25

BECKS

The next morning, I woke up with a smile on my face as I remembered what Adam and I had done, and sunlight streamed through the curtains into Adams' bedroom. He was still hugging me tightly to him, but he was sound asleep, resting peacefully.

I didn't want to wake him, but I needed to pee something serious, so as quietly and carefully as possible, I slid out of his embrace and tried to find the clothes I'd magicked from my body the night before. However, after a thorough and silent search, I came up empty.

Deciding I didn't have much of a choice, I grabbed the shorts I'd taken off before getting into Adam's bed, scurrying out of his room and into mine before anyone could see me.

I sought out my bathroom, not surprised at all to find that Brax was already gone from my bed, probably on another perimeter check if I had to guess.

That goyle woke up earlier than most, I'd noticed, that drive of his to continually be checking our surroundings for danger so strong that even sleep couldn't keep him from it.

Once I'd handled my unruly bladder, the shower beckoned me hard, and seeing as how everyone else was still asleep, I didn't deny my body what it needed right then.

The shower felt incredible, and when I was finished handling all of my hygienic requirements, I stood naked in front of the mirror for a second as I took in my appearance.

Something substantial had changed about me, but I couldn't quite place what it was exactly.

It wasn't something so obvious as a haircut or colored contacts. My wet hair was still just as long and brown as it'd always been, and my eyes, the same color blue.

Still, there was something undeniably different about the girl staring back at me.

She stood straighter, her eyes were smiling where they never really had before, and there was just this glow radiating from her that I couldn't explain.

I knew I had more power, and somehow, I knew I had even more control over it now than I'd ever had with less.

I also knew I'd been through a lot since the last time I'd gotten a really good look at myself, but even with all that, I still couldn't put my finger on what was so subtly different.

Shrugging away the discomfort of not knowing what I was picking up on, I made some loose-fitting shorts and a tank top appear on my body with a matching bra and panty set underneath, nearly slapping myself for forgetting I could've just magicked clothes on my body earlier, and headed to the kitchen to find food.

I was practically starving, the feelings I'd felt from that one Hell trial making me almost desperate for food and sustenance.

Taking a page out of Adam's breakfast routine, I thought I'd try my hand at making omelets since they seemed to be a pretty straight forward meal. I'd seen him make them a few times before, so my confidence in my ability to pull it off despite having never even cracked an egg in my life was pretty high.

I started by pulling out the peppers, onions, tomatoes, and mush-rooms I planned on stuffing inside the omelets. In short order, I had everything set up and ready to start prepping, even going so far as to have little bowls out and prepared to hold each of the chopped ingre-dients I was going to need.

As I was working, I couldn't help but smile and bask in the warmth of peace I felt seeping out of me and into the task.

I had these fantasized images flashing through my mind of white picket fences, four husbands, an elf-goyle familiar, and just a serene kind of peace I wished my life would turn out to have.

Making breakfast was nowhere near normal for me, much less making breakfast for everyone here, but I wanted to. The act felt like it *should* be normal. Like I was finally getting to do what most everyone else took for granted and got to do without thought or worry.

It was a normal thing for people to make food, and there I was, being all kinds of normal and enjoying every freaking second of it.

Eventually, when all the prep work had been completed, and the pan was heating up in front of me, I took a deep breath and bashed my first egg against the corner of the counter like I'd seen Adam do before.

"Ah, fuck," I said as the eggshell broke apart in shards, and the egg itself oozed out everywhere.

Quickly, I cleaned it up and threw all the remnants of my misstep into the trashcan, but when I was finally done with that, I realized the butter I'd put in the pan was now burnt beyond recognition.

"Fuck, fuck, fuck," I said to myself as I pushed the pan off the burner and put my hands on my hips.

'Calm down, it's okay,' I told myself around another large inhale. *'Just wipe out the pan and start again. You can still pull this off.'*

I let my self-talk guide me back into a better mood than the one I was about to slip into and set myself back up to start over.

However, when I was on my fourth egg cleanup detail, I was about ready to throw everything out into the ocean.

"It's just a fucking omelet!" I almost screamed as I threw my hands out and stared baffled at the stovetop.

Suddenly, hands grabbed each of mine from behind gently and pushed them down as Tyler's big arms wrapped around me. I didn't even need to wonder about who it was because our bond told me as soon as he touched me, that bond we shared getting stronger with every second his body stayed against mine.

"Having trouble?" he asked smoothly in my ear, and I couldn't stop the shiver that went through me when he said it.

I nodded, jerking myself out of any inappropriate thoughts that wanted to weigh in on what I could be doing instead of making breakfast, and answered him around a defeated sigh, "Yes. How can an omelet get on someone's nerves so bad?"

He chuckled darkly in my ear as he said, "Well, I happen to know a good remedy for nerves gone haywire if you're interested."

The innuendo and sin in his tone were undeniable, and there wasn't a cell in my body that didn't want to learn what he wanted to teach me.

I felt insatiable, like whether it was food, sex, or anything having to do with the guys, I just couldn't get enough and always needed more.

Being bolder than usual, I turned my head slightly toward him and rubbed my hand down his arm suggestively as I said, "Is that so?"

He perked up; I saw it. But he didn't stay surprised by what I'd said for longer than a heartbeat.

Tyler turned me around in his arms and stared down at me, a playful smile dancing at the corner of his lips. "Absolutely. There's nothing a few orgasms, and using the right pan can't fix."

"I wasn't using the right pan?" I questioned as I sent my gaze to the stove before all of his words sunk into my brain, and I turned to look back at him slowly.

"Orgasms, you say?" I asked with a smirk of my own, forgetting all about breakfast as Tyler chuckled some.

He picked me up then, causing a round of laughter to sound from both of us as he carried me over and placed me on an empty part of the counter, my arms instantly wrapping around his neck as we moved.

"Oh, yes," he said in between the kisses he was planting on my neck. "Orgasms can cure anything."

More laughter fell from me before a shocked gasp tore through my throat as he bit down hard on my neck.

Immediately, I was no longer in a stressed or playful mood. I was filled with ravenous want all over again, and as my hands clenched his biceps and his tongue slid out to soothe the bite he'd just inflicted, there was hardly anything left in me other than primal desire so intense I couldn't think straight.

On instinct alone, I grabbed Tyler's chin and forced his head sideways. As he let me expose his neck to me, I reveled in his vulnerability and sank my teeth into his flesh, marking my territory just as he had done to me.

His groan was loud and sent shivers straight through to my core, and as I sent my tongue across the smoothness of his neck to soothe the ache I'd caused, his fingers gripped my hips in a way that felt so possessive and strong, I nearly lost myself right there on the counter.

However, Tyler seemed to have a better idea since he pulled me down from the counter, roughly and unapologetically pulling my shorts and underwear down when my footing was solid.

No sooner had I stepped out of them than he was putting me back on the counter and grinning devilishly at me.

My legs were spread before him, and I knew I was remarkably open and exposed to him right then, but instead of feeling self-conscious about it, I felt empowered by it, by the way he was looking at me before he kissed me, as if his life depended on it.

I kissed him back just as fervently, but all too soon, he pulled away.

His grin was full of mischief as he pushed on my chest to make me lay back across the island.

The next thing I knew, his mouth was descending on my core.

Instantly, I gasped and dropped my head back to the counter as my eyes closed in sheer bliss from the movements of his tongue.

He licked and sucked, moaned, and dipped his hot tongue inside me, but it was when his touch turned almost delicate as he kissed my folds lightly that I lost all control of my body, sparks shooting through me.

Tyler pulled away then, and I was so upset that for a second, I almost wanted to slap him. However, he stood up to his full height and pulled me down from the counter faster than I could process what was going on before he turned me around, and my hands gripped the edge of the counter.

I heard his belt buckle loosen, and his pants drop to the floor right before I felt him rub his hard length right up against my folds roughly. He was rubbing his tip back and forth over the wet, most sensitive part of me, and within seconds, I came all over again, a feral moan spilling from my lips at the same time.

He slid into me then, his hands gripping my hips and pulling me down onto him hard.

At first, I was afraid it would hurt for some reason, but as his length slammed into me, all of that irrational fear disappeared and was replaced by euphoria instead.

I really wanted to see Tyler as he pounded into me, and I turned my head so I could look back over my shoulder at him, but as I saw his perfect body in my periphery, I nearly lost myself all over again.

However, keeping my head in that position was starting to hurt after a little bit.

I'd just decided to send my head back when I saw movement at the entrance to the hallway, and alarm spread through me.

Derrick stepped into the kitchen like he'd just been going about his morning as usual, but as he saw what Tyler and I were doing, his whole body went stiff while his eyes grew dark.

I was having a mini panic attack wondering whether we should stop, and I knew Tyler had seen him too, but it was as if having an audience only spurred Tyler on more, and his pace became unforgiving as Derrick stood there watching.

It was so erotic, so taboo, so fucking hot having Derrick watch, but that couldn't even come close to how it felt when he walked around to the other side of the island across from me and bent down. He leaned on his elbows as his gaze latched on and held mine, all while Tyler was fulfilling a fantasy I never even knew I should want.

The heat in Derrick's expression was so powerful I couldn't look away, and as one of his hands reached out to me where I was bent over the counter, I knew the heat in my eyes was matching his own.

His deft fingers slid into the neck of my tank top, easily gliding underneath the fabric of my bra to palm my breast in a way that was almost too possessive to reconcile, and as he squeezed, I came around Tyler like a madwoman.

A few thrusts later, Tyler found his own release, and Derrick let go of my breast before he stood up, walking over to the coffee pot as if nothing at all had just happened.

Meanwhile, I was still trying to catch my breath and wrap my mind around what I'd just experienced, but try as I might, my mind was utterly blown.

Slowly, I gathered my wits about me as both Tyler and I cleaned ourselves up and got dressed.

I was feeling a bit awkward and didn't know what to say exactly, but that went away quickly as Tyler came back over to me, trapping me in between him and the counter as he whispered in my ear, "That was fucking incredible, Becks."

Then stepping back some, he asked, "Feel better?" and instantly, a smile began to form on my face.

He seemed to take that as a 'yes,' since he immediately said, "See? I told you orgasms can fix anything."

Laughter spilled from me then, and if I wasn't mistaken, each of them was smirking too, which caused me to feel even better than I already was, a feat I hadn't exactly thought was possible until it happened.

It was as if these guys just took me to new heights and made it seem like that was as far as things could go before they blew my mind, taking me even higher.

And I fucking loved it. All of it.

"Do you want to tell me why your underwear showed up on my face last night?" Derrick asked a short time later over an unburnt breakfast Adam had made, and immediately, I felt blood seeping into my cheeks.

"That's not fair," Absinthe said as he dropped his hand to the table, "I only got her shirt."

My eyes spread open even further as I looked over to him, where he sat beside me, but before I could say anything, Tyler said, "I'm not complaining. I've got her sweet ass bra stashed under my pillow right now."

I was mortified. And turned on. And just... I couldn't really decide what I felt right then, but whatever it was, it was intense.

"I magicked them off of me last night," I said a bit sheepishly without going into too much detail about the fantastic time I'd had with Adam. "I guess my power sent them to you guys instead of keeping them where I wanted them."

"Awww," Absinthe said, a sweet smile playing at his lips. "Your power knew you weren't going to be joining us last night and sent us consolation prizes."

Suddenly, laughter sounded all around the table. Despite whatever prudish part of me wanted to take all the garments back on some sort of misguided principle, my feelings for each of the men around me won out as I laughed right along with them instead.

"I guess you guys can keep those then," I said eventually after everyone had sobered somewhat, but there was still a smile on my face as I said it.

Just then, Brax busted through one of the sliding glass doors, nearly breaking the glass in the process with how freaked out he was, but as he flew to a stop, taking all of us in, no words came from his mouth.

"What is it?" I asked as I rose to my feet without thinking.

"He's," was all Brax seemed to be able to get out as he pointed one of his little fingers toward the outside of the safe house.

Not knowing what to make of what was going on with him, I rushed outside with the guys following behind me.

I might not have known what I was seeing, but what I saw when I took in the horizon sent a shiver of dread through me so thick, I felt it in my bones.

Black smoky stacks of beings I couldn't name shot up into the sky in such overwhelming numbers that I instinctively knew if it wasn't stopped soon, the entire world was going to be overtaken by them.

"Who is that, Brax?" Derrick asked, and for a second, I couldn't understand what he was talking about, but as my eyes drifted from the sky down to the beach, I knew instantly what he'd meant.

There, standing in the sand staring up at us with a disgusting smile plastered across his face, was the shimmery man I'd seen in my gauntlet trying to influence Tina. I might not have had definitive proof, but I knew it was him, and as Brax spoke his name, an even larger, unprecedented amount of fear spread through me.

"That's Roland, my second charge," Brax said, horror filling his tone, "and those are all the damned souls that have ever been sentenced to the Void, spilling out from those portals."

To be continued...

ALSO BY CILLA RAVEN

Beholden To Balance

Initiate

Reign

Hunter

Defender

The Fae Bounties

Shameless Fae

Reckless Fae

Lost Savages MC

Wake

Take

Raging Heathens MC

Drifter

Prowler

Hallows

A Date With Death: Part One

Shared Worlds

Sneaky As A Fox

Lexi

HUNTER

BEHOLDEN TO BALANCE, BOOK 3

I sincerely hope you loved Hunter. If you enjoyed the book, I would really appreciate **an honest review** because they help so much! Thank you!

To get an immediate notification when I have a new release, please **sign up for my mailing list**!

To see the complete reading order for this series and to dive into all of my book worlds, **visit my website**!

ABOUT THE AUTHOR

Cilla Raven is an indie author that lives in Montana with her husband, children, and a few fur babies.

You can find all of Cilla's books, merchandise, and more on her **website**!

Love Cilla's books? **Join her mailing list** to be notified of new releases, giveaways, and more!

She'd love to have you join her **Facebook group**: *The Raven's Nest - A Cilla Raven Reading Group.* You'll get exclusive updates and teasers, live streams with Cilla over coffee, and all the funny memes you can stand. **Join now**.

www.ingramcontent.com/pod-product-compliance
Lightning Source LLC
Chambersburg PA
CBHW020604180626
46810CB00007B/2637